TWO FOR THE SHOW

SKYE WARREN

CHAPTER ONE

Eva

A WEDDING RECEPTION at the Met:

1. Stunning, eight-foot-high floral arrangements,

2. Priceless, world-class art,

3. And me, pregnant with Finn Hughes's baby.

Nobody knows. Not my family. Not Finn. Not a single person in this room has any idea that I'm carrying the baby of a man whose last words to me were *I wish I could say I'll miss you, but the truth is that I won't. In a few short years, I won't even remember you existed.*

What am I supposed to do with that?

Aside from keeping Daphne and Emerson's reception on track.

My sister's wedding is the perfect distraction.

I'm working with a James Beard award-winning chef for the canapés and booking the world-renowned violinist Samantha Brooks for the ceremony. Which means I don't have time to wonder about the small life growing inside me.

The Met is the perfect compromise to keep the peace with my parents. We had close family and friends only for the ceremony at Leo's church. And a large, lavish reception at the Met.

Emerson even went so far as to get baptized ahead of the wedding. I'm not sure if he meant it as an olive branch to the family for kidnapping Daphne or a symbol of his obsession.

Probably the latter.

Regardless of the reason, my parents seem to accept Emerson. My brothers do, too.

Which is a good thing. Peace is a transient thing in the Morelli family. I've learned to embrace it when it comes, even if it's fleeting. So I don't think about how my parents will freak out when they find out that I'm pregnant. And that the engagement with Finn Hughes is broken.

I don't think about the fact that I'll be the one to ruin the peace. I don't think about the fact that I'll have to tell them I'm pregnant.

And I don't think about how upset everyone will be.

We're almost at the finish line. Being the maid of honor makes everything easier, ironically. Plus, I could watch over everybody from the front of the church and make sure no scuffles broke out.

I could look at my family's faces and wonder if they'll all stroke out when they hear the news.

I was the one to coordinate the timing between the ceremony and the reception with the wedding planner, leaving plenty of buffer time for photos outside the church. It allowed me to get here first to make sure everything is perfect.

And, for the millionth time today, I wonder what I'm going to do.

Finn would want to know that I'm pregnant with his baby. Somehow, we both forgot to use a condom. And for whatever reason, Plan B didn't work. An ironic twist of fate. Somewhere a stork is laughing.

This is happening.

Finn would want to know, but he doesn't actually want a baby.

He was as clear as the crystal on the guest tables that he never wanted a child.

He *refused* to have a child, actually. Finn has valid reasons for that. I wouldn't dream of trying to convince him that his family's inherited illness was nothing.

But now the baby isn't a hypothetical. He or she is going to be our very real child. And no child of mine is going to feel the pain of being unwanted. No child of mine is a mistake.

The baby's barely the size of a pea, but my protectiveness feels as sharp as any of the cutlery gleaming near artfully folded napkins. I won't let Finn hurt the child by forcing us to stay separate *or* forcing us to stay close enough to see the depth of his disinterest.

Right on schedule, my family starts arriving at the reception.

Leo and Haley are first. They compromised on her bed rest situation. Leo agreed that Haley could go about her day normally, albeit while sitting or lying on the couch.

Haley agreed to let Leo carry her everywhere.

It's a classic Leo compromise, if you think about it.

There's no classic Finn compromise. Not on this issue. I'll have to decide this all on my own, for me and the baby.

I could lie to him. He might prefer it, actually.

I could announce that our engagement is off. Start rumors in Bishop's Landing that I'm seeing someone. Or several someones. Maybe I could pretend to sleep with a different man every night, the same way Finn was rumored to sleep with a different woman every night.

Then a few months down the road, I can tell everyone I'm pregnant and refuse to name the father.

The problem with that option is that Finn knows me. He got under my skin. He'd suspect that I didn't find a rebound guy to sleep with, much less twenty rebound guys. He would eventually know it was his child. And doesn't he have a right to know? Even if he doesn't want it. Even if it will hurt him to know.

My dad strides in through the gallery door, Mom close on his heels. He looks critically over the reception space and barks at a passing waiter for a drink.

"Dinner doesn't start for forty minutes," Mom points out in a cool tone.

"Good thing I'm not a lightweight," Dad growls. "Don't manage me."

"As if anyone could," she answers with a light party laugh.

The show has officially begun.

I station myself near the entrance to the gallery. More guests arrive, filling the space with warm chatter.

"We're having a polite conversation." Tiernan's low voice cuts through the door ahead of him. It's growly and menacing, which is normal for him. "I take it you've never been part of one before."

"I take it you never learned to fuck off before."

My disaster alarms go off. The target of Tiernan's sarcasm is Emerson's brother, Will Leblanc. Will looks coldly murderous. Tiernan's disgruntled. His girlfriend, Bianca, gives me big, worried eyes.

"Tiernan!" I approach my brother with a big, bright smile. "Go have a drink."

He opens his mouth as if to argue, but Bianca speaks first. "That is *such* a great idea. It looks beautiful in here, by the way! I especially love the hydrangeas. I've never seen them so big before."

Will hangs back, bristling. I put a hand on his elbow. He's my new brother-in-law. I don't know him that well, but he seems like a decent enough guy. "Don't mind Tiernan. Emotional days make him grumpy."

"Would a fistfight make him feel better? I wouldn't mind punching him."

"At least wait until after she throws the bouquet."

He snorts, his expression clearing. "Only because you asked. I appreciate everything you've done to smooth the way for Emerson. Your family isn't exactly…"

"Nice? Sane? Decent?"

"I was going to say *welcoming*," Will says, humor dancing in his blue-green eyes.

I like talking to Will. It's easier, at the moment, to talk to someone I don't know that well. Talking to my sisters, my brothers, my parents is hard because of the secret I'm keeping. Because of how badly I want to tell them the truth. Well, maybe not my parents. But Daphne, definitely. And my other siblings. I want their support right now, but I don't feel like I can have it.

Keeping secrets is nothing new to me. I'm even used to living with a broken heart.

It's over, sweetheart. We had a good time, but that's all this ever was.

Finn called what we had a fling. He chose words that he knew would cut deep. He was an asshole on purpose. I understood that, but the words still cut me. Since that night I've come up with a thousand comebacks that would destroy him.

It's a good thing he's not here.

Why would he be? A person like Finn wouldn't need to attend in person. Even if we weren't fake dating, he'd have to send a gift from Daphne and Emerson's Crate & Barrel registry.

In fact, I'm sure that's exactly what he did.

The room doesn't have space for him, anyway. I took him out of the seating arrangement and removed his preferences from the chef's list.

He was going to choose the vegetarian option.

Really? I said when I asked him. *You don't want Wagyu beef prepared by a team of chefs with a collective twenty Michelin stars?*

Finn had laughter in his eyes. *Anyone can cook beef, Morelli. Those two will make serious magic with plants.*

My father makes a speech to a crowd of people who are happily ensconced in their dinner. It's short, but in the middle he pauses. I hold the champagne glass I haven't sipped from to my chest.

I'm not the only one to notice the pause. My mother watches him, hawk-eyed, from her place at his side. An unruly, uneven part of me hopes that he'll cause some trouble.

Not really, of course. Not on Daphne's day.

I just want something to take the edge off. I'm cycling between angry and heartbroken and coolly focused every two minutes. If my father derails the reception, it'll take all my concentration.

My father clears his throat and raises his glass. He could say literally anything. Something cutting. Something cruel. "I wish you the best of everything, Daphne. To a long and happy life."

I sigh in relief as everyone claps.

Well, the wedding crisis was averted. My pregnancy crisis remains.

Except…it's not a crisis. I want the baby. The baby is mine. I'm going to have a baby.

Deciding what to tell Finn and when? That's the crisis.

I suppose it's only a matter of choosing the method of communication. A letter seems…overly formal. A text message would seem like a cruel joke. Maybe I can send a carrier pigeon?

Calling him is probably the right thing to do, but I don't want to hear him shut down. I don't want to hear him say that he doesn't want this baby and will have nothing to do with it. I'd rather get there first.

I'd rather tell him that I'm handling it on my own and that he doesn't need to be involved. That I don't want him involved, and I won't let him near the baby.

You don't like charming men, remember? And that's the one thing I am: charming.

He wasn't charming when he broke up with me.

I still can't bring myself to feel okay with preemptively kicking him out of the baby's life. Finn was cruel. That doesn't mean I have to be. Even if Finn doesn't deserve the baby, the baby deserves a father. And the truth is… I know that Finn would be a great father. He's funny and patient and sweet.

Except for when he broke up with me.

That knifelike protectiveness surges up again. I'll be polite since he's the father of my child, but I won't be weak. I won't be small and heartbroken the way I was after Lane.

Emerson's brother Sinclair pats him on the shoulder on his way to make his speech. His work as an investigative journalist and extreme sportsman keeps him busy. We've chatted a couple of times at Emerson's house. I've read a few of his long form pieces, and they're very good.

I wonder if he'll be as eloquent in person.

He lifts the mic and clears his throat. Murmurs in the room die off, and Sinclair nods toward Emerson. His blue eyes look emotional, though his voice is steady. "Hey, Em."

"Hey," Emerson says from his spot at the sweetheart table with Daphne. This gets a laugh from the guests.

"I'm going to talk about you to all these people, if that's okay."

Emerson takes Daphne's hand and gestures at Sinclair to continue.

"Great." Sinclair sticks his other hand in his pocket. "For those who don't know, my name is Sinclair. I'm Emerson's older brother. Since you're all here, I'm betting you know that Emerson has occasionally dabbled in the art scene."

Another laugh goes up.

"Ever since I've known him, my brother has always been the kind of person who seeks out beauty. You could put him on the ugliest street corner in Brooklyn, and he'd notice that the raindrops there reflected all the colors of the neon lights. He'd tell you to look closer until you could see it."

Emerson stares at his brother like he's never heard anything so inaccurate about himself. Or maybe so accurate.

"Emerson sees beauty everywhere he goes, and maybe that's why he's so particular about what he wants. You can't impress this guy with run-of-the-mill *pretty*. You need to be fucking breathtaking to steal his heart. Only one person has ever done that, and that's Daphne."

Daphne blushes. One of Emerson's hands is in both of hers.

That's how I'd hold Finn's hand if he wanted a baby.

God, it would be so much easier if he just…wanted a baby. If he just wanted a family.

If he just wanted me.

My throat closes. I was foolish to fall for Finn Hughes, but I'm outright ridiculous to wish I'd stolen his heart, too.

"Here's how I know they're perfect for each other," Sinclair says. "Fun fact about Emerson: he surfs every day, all year. Daphne, I'm sorry to say, has terrible balance. But she goes with him anyway."

Someone at one of the middle tables says *aww*.

"No, you don't understand." Sinclair holds up a hand. "This woman is terrified of decent-sized waves. One day this summer I watched her scream all the way back to the shore. She was still out there on Emerson's board with him."

Warm applause. Daphne leans in and kisses Emerson's cheek. I use the pause to look out over the tables.

Finn stands at the entrance to the gallery.

My heart stops.

He came.

Anger stomps down on that thought like a pointed high heel. How dare he come here? How dare he show up like nothing happened? Like we're *something* to each other?

We're not. We're nothing.

He wears a tux that looks incredible on him. It emphasizes his broad shoulders and his lean hips. A few women notice him, too. It's hard not to. It's like a young Brad Pitt just walked into the room. Even silent he radiates a presence. He inclines his head at me, a tacit greeting.

I'm the first to look away.

Sinclair continues his speech. "Look. Love is scary as hell. I'm proud of you, Em, for having the courage to love Daphne more than you've ever loved anything else. And Daphne, I think you'd agree with me that Emerson deserves the world. So congratulations on being absolutely everything to him." He raises his champagne glass. "To love and bravery."

Daphne has tears of joy in her eyes.

I have tears in my eyes, too. Sinclair's speech moved me to pissed-off, heartbroken tears that I won't let fall. Not in front of Finn freaking Hughes.

I can feel his eyes on me as I watch Daphne dab at her eyes with a tissue, laughing at the same time. As Emerson leans in to kiss her, not seeming to care about the five hundred guests. As another happily ever after begins right in front of me while my heart breaks again.

CHAPTER TWO

Finn

I DIDN'T COME here to get sucker-punched by a wedding toast.

I probably deserve it. It feels wrong and intrusive to be here. Eva and I agreed to fake a relationship, but showing up at her sister's wedding reception strikes me as dishonest given that I was supposed to be her plus one. And given the way I spoke to her.

It's over, sweetheart.

I'd made up my mind not to come; then at the last minute I got dressed and drove here.

I feel like an asshole, looking at Eva. And I also feel like I've come home. Like I can finally breathe again now that I'm in the same room. Five hundred people have taken over a section of the Met. She's across the room. It's still better than being without her.

Eva faces forward, not looking at me. Her brothers are getting up to make speeches. Leo gets choked up in the middle of his and abandons the entire thing. He finishes by handing Emerson an envelope and giving a toast to art.

Carter takes the microphone from Leo and pats his shoulder. "We're all going to forget what we've just seen," he intones, and then he tells a story about how Daphne started out sketching and drawing and painting everything she could see or imagine. He'd study science, and she'd study the world. It took her years of careful study to find her true obsession, but she never gave up. "And now you found him," Carter says. "I always knew you would."

Frankly, it's awful. The little hints of their family life make me feel closer to Eva and miles away. I want her so much that it hurts.

For sex purposes, obviously. And also for this life that she has. Her family is overbearing and dysfunctional and intense. Sometimes I think they need to learn some goddamn boundaries. But they belong to Eva, and she's part of them, too. I want to be by her side when she's in the thick of it.

I won't abandon you. No matter what.

That's what she said to me. And what did I do? I broke up with her. Threw her out.

Daphne and Emerson rise from their table.

It's time for cake.

I hang back until they've cut a slim piece from a cake subtly designed with an ocean theme. Even at a distance, I know Eva had something to do with it. Ivory fondant gives the impression of light coming through water. A spray of edible pearls curves down one side.

The photographer swoops in to capture the moment. Then waiters fan out among the tables, and I make my approach.

Daphne's smile gets wider when she sees me. "Finn! Hi!"

"Congratulations, Daphne. Emerson." I shake his hand. "Beautiful reception."

"I'm so glad you could make it." Daphne clasps her hands in front of her. "Eva said you weren't going to be able to come. Is your dad feeling better?"

"I hope he is," Eva says from directly at my side. Her mouth is soft with concern, but her dark eyes are sharp. She could make the accusation right now. *You shouldn't be here.*

"Much better." By this point in my life, the lie is automatic. The feelings underneath it are not.

They're a goddamn mess. Eva covered for me, even after I was a bastard to her. "I'll let him know you were thinking of him."

"Is there anything I can get for you?" Eva's tone is distant, as if I'm just another one of the guests. Death by a thousand cuts. "If you're hungry, I can have a dinner plate brought out."

I give her a classic Finn Hughes smile. "I'm here to celebrate and enjoy the company. Don't worry about me."

"Oh, I wouldn't." Eva laughs, but she doesn't take her eyes off me. Is it pain or hatred glittering there? It reminds me of a broken champagne glass.

"We all know that's not true. You're the best hostess of our time. An expert in worrying about party guests and making everything perfect."

"Some things are beyond even me."

"I doubt that."

"Well, don't." Eva's tone is as light and steely as barbed wire. "I have my limits like everybody else."

Daphne's beaming, hardly paying attention to our conversation. Her husband, on the other hand, sees everything. His eyes move between me and Eva with sharp intensity. I don't love the feeling that he knows exactly what he's looking at.

Torture, in the middle of a wedding reception.

But his face stays calm. If he's noticed and understood the tension between us, he doesn't say a word about it.

"Eva." Daphne leans toward her. "Do you think—" Someone calls Daphne's name from a nearby table. "I'll ask you later. It was really good to see you, Finn. Don't forget to dance with Eva, okay?"

Daphne and Emerson are pulled away, leaving me with Eva.

It's hell to be this close to her and not kiss her. It's hell to know that this isn't fixable. It's hell to know I can't leave. Not until I've tried.

She takes a tiny step closer and lifts her chin. "I'm sorry." The apology is frosty. I'm probably imagining the layer of warmth underneath. "I didn't know what else to say."

About my father being ill. It's technically true. The irony is not lost on me that she's apologizing when I was the asshole, even if she's being terse and polite.

I know I should leave her alone. I can't bring myself to leave.

I wave off her apology. "How have you been?"

Dark eyes skim over my face, and Eva purses

her lips. There's no current of flirtation between us now. The night I stole her from the Morelli Mansion, we were a team. It was us against the world. Now there's an ache in my chest like my heart has been stabbed, repeatedly, with one of the dinner forks.

"I've been well, Finn. Thanks."

It's so dismissive it kills me. More than dismissive. This is polite avoidance from Eva Morelli. She's probably still pissed at me.

That's fair.

"Any plans for the holidays?"

Eva looks away, holding her champagne glass close to her body. There's about an inch in the glass. She doesn't take a sip. "I'd imagine we'll have the usual get-togethers."

"I'm available to help with the mince pies." I'll never forget working with her in the big kitchen at the Morelli Mansion. She wouldn't stop until everything was perfect. I just wanted an excuse to be near her.

She gives a short, shallow laugh. "We'll have that under control. I wouldn't want you to lose any sleep over it. You should enjoy the holidays to the fullest."

Elsewhere, she means. Not at the gala hosted by her family. Not with her.

This is more than Eva being distant. She's being…cagey. Vague on the details. Making a point of discouraging me from coming anywhere close.

Is she dating someone else?

Jealousy rises. It's ridiculous for me to be jealous, but I am. I saw Alex Langley among the guests. That was probably Sarah Morelli's doing. Eva's not interested in him.

But the fact is, someday she *will* be with someone. And I'll have to watch.

I'll have to watch her be conspiratorial with him and familiar with him and happy with him.

I'll have to watch until I don't.

"The champagne's flowing freely tonight. You must have figured out a way to make sure you never run out."

Her eyes come back to mine, and there it is. The sparkle I saw there on the night I asked her out. The heat. And yes, the happiness. It's gone in an instant, but I *saw* it.

I can feel it between us. It's like a physical pull. I want to take her hand and tug her out of the Met and into my car. Maybe if I went through the steps we took that night, found her someplace illicit and hidden to take her, we could get that feeling back.

Because it was building. It was becoming something strong and unshakable and goddamn delicious.

"Finn." Sarah Morelli sweeps in, obvious delight on her face. "We were so sorry to hear your father wasn't feeling well. I trust he recovered, if you're here?"

"Yes, absolutely." I lean down to kiss her cheek. "He insisted that I come tonight. *You don't let a woman like Sarah Morelli down,* he said."

Sarah laughs, dismissing this with a wave even as her face flushes. "Of course you're here for Eva. Breathtaking, isn't it? I think she's surpassed me at hosting events."

"She could only do that because she learned from the best." I wink at Sarah. "One detail got overlooked, though. She hasn't asked me to dance."

"Eva, you must. This is the best wedding of the season. Let's toast, and then you'll take your fiancée to the dance floor."

"Oh, no thank you, Mama."

Sarah rolls her eyes, smiling. "You and your newfound sobriety. It's all right to relax a little once the speeches are over, Eva."

Sobriety?

Eva hasn't taken a single sip of her champagne. Awareness whispers across the back of my neck like a woman blowing on a pair of dice.

Something else is going on here.

The music kicks up in volume. Eva hands off her champagne glass to Sarah like she's been caught out with it. "I like this song," she says, her tone bright and cheery and fake. "You're right. We should dance."

She takes my hand and pulls me onto the dance floor.

Eva Morelli is hiding something.

Whether that's a new boyfriend, I haven't the faintest clue. All I know is that I'm being led onto the dance floor for a reason.

I know it, but I don't make any move to stop her. It feels too damned good to have my hand in hers. It's a balm to put my hand on her waist and pull her close.

It feels too good.

"I know you're doing this to distract me," I murmur against her temple.

Eva curls her fingers through mine, finding the beat of the song. "Is it working?"

"Yes."

CHAPTER THREE

Eva

FINN HAD NO reason to be suspicious before. He does now.

Turning down the toast was a very smooth move. He knows I'm distracting him, and letting me do it.

I'm letting him pull me close as the music gets louder. My cheeks feel red-hot with anger and a touch of panic. His hands at my waist steady me.

It's a real dilemma, because I don't want him to back away. I've missed him. Being close to him. The masculine scent of him.

And I can't believe he'd show up here.

You've made another mistake, Eva. I'll forgive you for it. The question is whether you'll forgive yourself.

I told Finn Hughes the secret I've kept from

almost everyone, and he used it against me. I want to drag him out of the Met by his collar and shout those words back at him through a megaphone.

I can't. Distractions only work if you commit to following through.

He tugs me closer, moving with the beat. I could end it now. Tell him in a clipped, icy tone that I'm pregnant with his baby, I'm keeping it, and he can leave me the hell alone.

It would create a black hole in the middle of Daphne's wedding day. Finn would be shocked and hurt, and even if he managed to leave quietly, I would know what I'd done.

So what? A tiny voice whispers in the back of my mind. *He hurt you first.*

I straighten in Finn's arms so I can see his eyes. He searches my face, looking for something. Answers, probably. Or forgiveness.

He's not getting either one.

"How is Hemingway doing?"

Finn gives me a shallow nod, his expression clearing. He takes his family responsibilities seriously. I can't fault him for that. My heart squeezes, guilty. I'm using a question about his family to hide another kind of family responsibility. One he doesn't know he has.

And one I have every right to hide. His gor-

25

geous face isn't going to guilt me into anything.

We turn, gliding through the other couples. "Hemingway has officially settled in at home with us. He's doing virtual school for the rest of the year as a trial run."

"How did that go over with your parents?"

Finn huffs a breath. "My mother threw an absolute fit."

"She doesn't agree with the living situation?"

"She has some real concerns."

"Isn't she traveling most of the time?" That's the reason Hemingway was at boarding school, and the reason Finn is the one in charge of his education. Finn's mother is away, and his father is also away, albeit not physically.

"Some of them are the same concerns I have. Attending online school means Hemingway's going to miss out on socialization. I'm worried he could get depressed, being around our dad instead of kids his age." Finn sets his mouth into a determined line. "It's what he wants, though. I owe him a trial run."

"Then I'm sure it'll all turn out."

"He might not tell me if it doesn't."

"Why wouldn't he?"

A shrug. "Because he already admitted that he wants it. Even if he realizes it's awful, he might not say anything. Sunk-cost fallacy."

"Doesn't seem very likely to me."

Finn's eyebrows draw together. Screw him for being so hopeful about this conversation. "Doesn't it?"

"He's not as alone as you think he is. Hemingway has you." I say it with an edge. I watch the words land. *Your brother has you, and you're awful.*

The corners of his mouth turn down. "That's right."

I wish I had him, in spite of myself. I wish he could want me the same way instead of being so obstinate. "And how are you? How is the charming Finn Hughes doing?"

This time, a little breath goes out of him.

You think you love me? No. You don't even like *me. You don't like charming men, remember?*

"Just fine." His easy tone is proof that he's lying. "I'm busy running the company. Busy being head of the family. Same as always."

Same as always, except everything is different now. Just *how* different, I haven't told him.

His hand tightens on my waist. Finn's eyes linger on mine. It's an intimate communication. I can feel all the conflicts he's facing in the way he moves. Tension, from worrying about his family and himself.

Maybe even guilt, from the way things ended between us.

And desire.

His touch is a potent reminder of how good we were together. When I was alone with Finn, the rest of the world didn't weigh so much. My body felt alive and alight for the first time in so long.

I could lose myself in him.

I won't let that happen. I'm not going to give in.

His masculine scent fills my next breath, and I lose the battle with myself. Memories of his naked body over mine collide with me at the same time. Heat rushes to my cheek and my nipples tighten under my dress.

Finn's eyes darken.

He notices.

One breath, and we're not just dancing. Not anymore. He's moving my body sensually against his.

He's having a reaction, too. I can feel how hard he is.

How much he wants me.

It's hot, and it hurts. The heat between us is a siren song. It makes me want to lean into it, into him, and I do.

I've been longing for this contact from the second I left his house.

He didn't have to come here tonight. Now that he has, I'm going to show him what he was missing. I want him to feel as lonely and bereft as I do. It's not kind, but it's true.

Finn lets out a harsh breath and allows himself to pull me closer. He shudders when my hips make contact with his cock, gritting his teeth to hide it. We're riding the line of *very inappropriate for a wedding reception.* It's basically sex on the dance floor.

That was when we were at our best. When we were fucking each other. When everything seemed like it could be a wonderful, secret game. A happy one.

Now it's a fight. I want to prove I don't need him. He wants to prove...

I don't know what.

He's handsome. A confident dancer. I feel sensual in his arms. Wanting him feels like a warm, physical weight. If things hadn't ended between us, we could run away together. Not to an illicit poker club, but at least to a dark alcove. Somewhere we could put our hands on each other in private.

Except it's not how it used to be. I feel

bruised, and he's wary. The safety of his arms has been transformed into pure tension.

Does it have to be *this* hard? Honestly, I'd hoped it wouldn't be. Finn smells so good. Breathing him in only makes me want him more.

Fake dating used to be fun and sexy. Now it's painful. We're at my sister's wedding, surrounded by people on the dance floor, and none of them know how jagged and complicated our relationship has become.

Well, Emerson seems to know. I saw the way he looked between us. The one advantage is that I don't think he cares. To him, we're just another piece of art. Daphne, though? It nearly killed me to see her so happy for me when I'm raging at him on the inside.

I want to hurt him and dismiss him. And I want to take him someplace private and tear off his clothes.

He lets out a breath near my temple. "You feel good."

"Oh?" My arms settle on his shoulders. It's difficult to think in all this heat. "Is that why you decided to show up?" I sound more acerbic than I planned.

"I don't know." Finn smiles, and it breaks my heart. "One minute I was at home. The next I was putting on my tux. Then I was here. There wasn't much conscious thought involved. And with you this close, I don't know how there could be."

The beat of the song gets heavier. For a few moments, I let it happen. I let myself forget. The reception. The guests. The secrets. It all disappears, and I move with him.

There are so many layers of movement. Each one reminds me what he was like when we could be together. *Alone* together. Understanding each other.

"Finn, I—"

Abruptly, the song ends. A cheer goes up. Then laughter. The guests transition right into a wild rendition of the Chicken Dance.

"Jesus," Finn says, under his breath. He keeps his hands firmly on my waist and guides me to the side of the floor. We duck people's arms and elbows.

My skin tingles from how close he is. From how close I came to blurting out that I'm pregnant.

On the other side of the dance floor, Leo and Haley stand close together. He's at her back, his arms reaching forward to support her belly. She beams while they watch the other people dance, swaying slightly. My chest aches. Jealousy and happiness war with each other. I'm never going to have that with Finn.

In the opposite corner, Daphne glows. She and Emerson stand off to the side of an artist they hired to paint a scene from their wedding in real time. Her eyes are huge and bright. *It's beautiful,* he says to her, but anyone can see that no painting will ever be more beautiful than Daphne. Not to him.

"How did all the planning go?" Finn asks. He's been following my eyes around the room.

"It was a nightmare."

"Really?"

"Yes. It was far less complicated than I wanted it to be. Daphne was an easy bride."

Finn's eyes narrow. "*Less* complicated? You think it should have taken more of your time?"

"I like a challenge, now and then."

His jaw works. He didn't really have the right to make comments about my family before. Now that we're not together, he certainly doesn't. It won't be much longer until that family includes our child, and he sure as hell can't comment on that. Not unless he's going to say that he's changed his mind.

"I think Daphne will be relieved when it's over."

Hazel eyes return to mine. "Is that how you'll feel after your wedding?"

The question is so loaded I feel it in my bones. Finn put the slightest emphasis on *your*. We weren't actually engaged. It was all pretend. And yet thinking of a wedding that's mine and not Finn's too feels wrong.

"I don't know." I smooth my hair. "I imagine I'll feel relieved, but a little sad that it's over. I know she'll be glad she doesn't have to argue with Mom and Dad anymore. Not until there's a baby shower, anyway."

His face darkens at the memory of the last baby shower, but Finn doesn't say anything.

For a guy who dismissed me in the cruelest way possible, he's obviously struggling. Walking a fine line between not wanting to upset me and not wanting me to be upset.

In reality, it's both of us. I'm not sure how he's going to take this news. I don't want to upset him. And I don't want him to be upset.

The question of who has the right to upset the other person is well behind us now.

A new song starts. More guests move around us. Finn pulls me into his side to keep me out of their way, as if he doesn't want anything else to touch me.

At one of the nearby tables, a baby cries.

The sound cuts straight to the quick. I turn my head without thinking. I'm sure the baby is fine. Safe with its parents. But it tugs at my heart.

I drop my hand to my belly without thinking. I know the baby is mainly just cells at this point. I know it can't be comforted by my touch, or by anything else. It doesn't know that somewhere, another child is crying.

I'll fix it, I think.

And then—

Shit.

I move my hand away, as casually as possible, and face Finn.

His eyes are wide with shock. With horror. He saw what I did. His hand is at my waist, so he felt me turn. Felt me respond to that cry.

They go down to my belly and come back up to my face.

"Finn. Listen to me."

"Eva." He steels himself. "What the fuck?"

CHAPTER FOUR

Finn

I MEAN THOSE words with every scrap of my soul. What the fuck. What the *fuck*.

Eva cannot be pregnant.

A suggestion presents itself. *It's not yours. She's pregnant with another man's baby. It's fast, but it's not impossible.*

I know it's not true. I know how carefully she tried to protect her broken heart. She doesn't just jump into bed with anyone. It was a miracle she left her parents' house with me at all. Every second Eva Morelli gave to me was a gift after how devastated she was about Lane.

And I threw it back in her face, like a complete bastard. I sent her home, where presumably she discovered…this.

I didn't do this. I can't have done this. We

cannot have done this thing.

Getting a woman pregnant is one thing I swore I'd never do. Getting married? Having a family? Never. And not for my own sake, but theirs.

Well, I'm not avoidant like Eva. I don't sweep things under the rug. I don't hide the truth from myself. Not ever.

"Finn." Her hand grips my elbow.

I saw the way her face changed when that baby cried. I saw how her fingertips brushed her belly, which is still flat.

No.

I tuck her hand into my elbow and propel her away from the dance floor. I'm gentle but firm. We're going to talk about this. We're going to get to the bottom of how exactly this happened.

"Finn, stop." There's a note of panic in her voice. She was trying to keep this from me. I was right. She was acting strange earlier. Being avoidant. Not because she's angry with me...or not *just* because she's angry. It's because of the...

I can't even think the word.

Not now. Not in front of all these people.

"Eva," someone calls.

I don't know who it is. One of her mother's thousand friends or acquaintances. It doesn't matter. Nothing matters except getting to a place where I can have a real conversation with Eva about the disaster that's about to decimate our lives.

She waves, tugging at my arms. "An issue with the dessert table." Eva gives them a little laugh, as if to say *weddings, right?* "I'll be back in a few minutes."

Whoever it is seems to believe her. No footsteps follow after us. A problem with the dessert table. Jesus. This is the end of the world, and she's smoothly making up excuses about frosted cookies and macarons.

She's covering for me because I'm steering her out of here like a maniac.

I know I am, but I can't stop.

There are so many people here. They form a crowd, even in the large space. Impossible to see the paintings on the walls at the Met. We turn corner after corner until we're in a relatively secluded gallery.

It's not secluded enough. I can still hear the music from Daphne's wedding. Still hear the chatter of voices. It'll have to be enough.

A painting of a mother with her young daughter stares at us from the wall. They're peaceful together. Happy. The mother is bent over her sewing, and her daughter leans in close.

I take her shoulders and line her up in front of it. "Eva."

"What."

"*Eva.*"

"Is there something you want to tell me?"

She lifts her chin, her eyes flashing. Eva doesn't look the least bit fragile now. She's all Morelli intimidation and scorn. "Absolutely not."

I swear to fucking God, I'm at the end of my rope. The very end. Look. There it goes. But Eva's being mulish. I can see it in the set of her beautiful, stubborn mouth.

"Eva."

Nothing.

Words aren't enough for all the fear and anger of this moment. It hums between us, along with our past. We have a past now, Eva and me. We got under each other's skin.

God, I wanted her. From the moment I saw her in that room, I wanted her.

I want her now.

I miss her like hell, and this thing she's not telling me? It doesn't stop how much I ache for her.

I lean in for a kiss.

Eva turns her head away.

It's a cold shock. I should have expected it.

Her throat tenses with every breath she takes. Being shut out like this hurts like knowing your own expiration date. My lungs momentarily stop working, but I need air to keep fighting with her. I'll go down fighting.

"Come on, Morelli. You weren't this shy on the dance floor."

"I don't want anything to do with you." So simple. So precise. Everybody gives the Morelli brothers credit for being sharp as knives, but Eva's slipped one between my ribs. I saw it coming. I didn't stop it.

"So you're pissed at me. That's not a reason to lie."

She turns to look at me, keeping her head against the wall. "It's over, sweetheart."

I know I put the weapon in her hands, but god*damn*. I trap her chin on instinct. Eva glares at me, breathing hard. It's not over. That's the argument. "You don't want to kiss me? I want to kiss you."

Her mouth becomes a thin, angry line, but she doesn't move. It's not an invitation.

But it's not a refusal.

I press my advantage and kiss her despite the fury in her eyes.

There, a voice says. *There.* She tastes soft and good and melts into me like I didn't break up with her like an asshole. Like I didn't cross every line we'd drawn in the sand.

Eva's body moves into mine just like it did on the dance floor. She's sweet and sensual and a queen, all at once. Her arms slide around my neck. Her hips press into mine. Her back meets the wall beside that painting of a mother with her child.

There's no father in the painting.

I drown that thought in her kiss. Lose myself in it. I lick her and bite her with a thorough concentration, as if we have all the time in the world. The reception can end, for all I care. Museum staff can usher people out at the end of the night.

Eva makes a frustrated sound against my mouth. I recognize it. I've spent enough hours in her bed to know that it means she wants more.

I want more, too, and I'm going to have it. I came to this reception, I pulled her into this gallery, and I'm going to give her what we both want.

I let myself sink deeper into her mouth. Into the even pressure of her body against mine. The tiny rolls and bucks of her hips, even for a kiss.

Eva wants me to fuck her. She's practically begging now, with every move she makes and every sound.

I nuzzle the side of her neck. Nip at the lobe of her ear. Make her shiver. This is simple cause and effect. This stretch of skin, here, makes her hips roll. This tug of her lip draws out a sound. It's everything.

I kiss her harder, exploring her. Memorizing her. I won't forget this. I don't know how I could. It's the taste of perfection. It's the taste of heat and home.

It's her.

I lean down close to her ear. "Eva."

"I hate you."

"I don't hate you. I *want* you."

One sharp breath, and she breaks down.

Her first sob is just the beginning. Eva keeps them quiet, so that they don't bother anyone else, but they shake her entire body.

Fuck.

It's true.

I knew it was. I knew from the moment I saw her fingertips touch her belly. But somehow I thought it might be something else. Somehow, I held out hope.

Eva remains stiff and upright until I gather

her into my arms, holding her tight. Her shoulders shake. I run my hands up and down her back, shushing her while my own pain breaks over me.

I didn't want this to be true. I didn't want this to happen to her. The way Eva sobs is just a precursor. That's all having a baby with me can ever be—devastating.

She's pregnant with my baby.

I never wanted this. Not just for me, but for Eva. She deserves a lifetime of happiness, and instead she has a ticking clock.

My throat closes. Eva's still crying. I hope she doesn't notice that I've temporarily lost the ability to say a damn thing. I just learned about this pregnancy a few minutes ago, and already it's a knife in my heart. *Not my baby,* a voice cries from somewhere deep down. *Not my son. Not my child.*

I can't do this here. Not at the fucking Met. Not at a wedding reception. I can't.

I kiss Eva through her tears. It's a salty, desperate kiss, and Eva throws her arms around my neck and kisses me back. Her shoulder bumps the painting of the mother and daughter.

I'm hard at the touch of her lips. My body wants Eva more than it will ever want grief.

I want Eva more.

And…I need her. I've been miserable since I sent her out of my house. Even animals know when their pair is gone. Horses sure as hell know.

Sex isn't a solution. It's the only thing we have. We're still alive and aware enough to have it.

Her dress doesn't fight me when I push it up to her hips. Slide her panties to the side. I barely get my zipper undone before she's begging wordlessly into my mouth and trying to climb me.

I'm a gentleman. I hold her up against the wall. I thrust in slow.

Eva's wet.

That's the goddamn miracle of humanity, isn't it? That she can still want to fuck me after what I've done to her. After what I've done to both of us.

What I've done disappears into her slick heat. It disappears into fucking her up against the wall. She clenches around me, her body getting hotter. Fingernails test the skin near my collar, searching for more. She gets it. Tiny crescents dig in under my shirt.

I'm not sure which of us is trying to fuck the other one harder. Eva works herself down over me. I'm frantic to fuck into her. With my hands supporting her ass I can feel every move she makes.

It's wonderful.

Eva's a rose pushing up through a crack in the sidewalk. Us, together—we're safe harbor when a storm's coming in over the ocean. It doesn't matter that the storm is here already. It doesn't matter that we made it ourselves.

Chapter Five

Eva

FINN KISSES THE side of my neck, hot and expert. That's the playboy in him. I'm lightheaded from sobbing while we fuck up against a wall in the Met.

I don't care that it's wrong. I don't care that we both have reputations to protect. I've spent my life keeping my family from imploding, and right now, I don't care.

The confident playboy disappears. Finn drops his head onto my shoulder and fucks me like it's the only way he can stay alive.

I feel that way, too.

It's ironic, isn't it? We don't have to worry now. He doesn't have to fumble for a condom because I'm already pregnant with his baby. His worst nightmare has already come true. It's alive, right in front of him.

He changes the angle of my hips, and the contact with my clit sweeps away every coherent thought. Finn grunts when I start to come. He holds me down against him. Harder than before. He makes a sound of pure relief.

"Feels good," he mumbles against my jaw.

I turn my head and kiss him.

Yes. It does. It feels good to have him lose himself inside me. It always does.

Maybe it'll be okay. Maybe this nightmare is almost over. We have a chance. That's all we've ever needed.

Hope rises like champagne bubbles as the moment comes down. The sounds of Daphne's reception filter into the gallery. Finn's tension filters back into his body. I wish he'd let it go. Turn into the good man he was, right up until the last moment. Turn back into the Finn Hughes I fell for.

We untangle ourselves from each other, and from the wall. I rearrange my dress. He unbuttons his jacket, smooths his shirt, and re-buttons it.

Both of us step away from the wall and face the art. Where's the father of the child in this painting? Is he in the next room? At work?

Is he dead?

Or is the painting from his perspective? Is he meant to be the viewer, looking at his wife and their child?

I've seen a print of this painting before. Almost everyone has. But I've never thought about it quite like this. I've never had the original hang on a wall nearby while I have an emotional breakdown in the arms of one Finn Hughes.

I could keep sobbing. Lately, I seem to be an endless well of tears. Instead, I take deep, even breaths and pat at my hair. I put my thoughts back in order the way I rearranged my dress.

Finn slides his hands into his pockets. He hasn't taken a step away from me, but there's a new distance between us.

My stomach sinks. "Finn."

He gives a quick shake of his head, like he's been lost in thought. "We'll marry, of course."

It's a slap in the face. I jerk back from the impact and the pain. Finn doesn't notice. He's not even looking at me. He scans the painting of the mother and daughter for another beat, then turns absently toward me.

"*Finn*."

"We'll make the announcement next month. It won't be too close to Daphne's wedding, but it'll leave us time to marry before the birth."

Anger floods back in. It could light this gallery on fire. "Ideally before I'm showing, right?"

"Yes, of course."

"So you're planning on a short engagement."

"Obviously." Finn's brow furrows, like I'm being deliberately obtuse. It's another slap in the face. How could he think this was the right way to do this? How could he think I would want this? "As far as everyone knows, we're already engaged, so a relatively hasty wedding wouldn't be out of line."

"Excellent plan. Did you have a venue in mind?"

"Your family's church, I would guess."

"You're not Catholic."

Finn waves this off. "You are. And I'm sure there are things to be done. Permission from the priest or whatever."

"My father will be thrilled."

Either he doesn't notice my brittle tone or doesn't care that I'm holding back the urge to slap *him* until he comes to his senses. I wouldn't actually do that, but the moment calls for something dramatic.

Instead, I double down on icy composure. It's served me very well in the past. A voice whispers that it won't serve me well now, but it's too late.

I'm committed to being angry. I can't help being hurt. Every word out of his mouth hurts more.

"That's an advantage, then. I wouldn't want him to make things difficult."

"My mother will be beside herself."

"I'll talk to her," Finn says.

"She'll be so happy. Four weddings in one year? That means she gets four chances to be the center of attention."

"I'm happy to let her be the center of attention. I'm sure she'll want to be involved in the planning."

"Oh, I'm *absolutely* sure. You'll be the one to break the news to her, then?"

"Whatever makes the transition the smoothest."

The *transition*. Like he's moving me to another branch of his company. Like he's suggesting in the most callous way that our fake engagement turn into a real one.

My hurt is folding into white-hot rage. I've known for a long time that men aren't to be trusted. Rich men and Constantines in particular. I'm angry at myself for allowing even a second of false hope, but I'm furious with him for letting me lead him down this path.

A better woman would put a stop to it.

Would plant her feet and raise her eyebrows and say *are you serious right now?* She would make him understand how awful he was being.

Except I want him to see it for himself.

I won't accept anything less.

"What about the honeymoon?"

The corner of Finn's mouth turns down. "I can't be away from my father for very long. Paris for a week. I have a place in the Virgin Islands. Something for the *Sunday Styles* section in the Times. We'll keep it simple."

"Simple, but backed up by photo evidence."

"That's right."

I let out a disbelieving laugh. "What will your mother think?"

"She'll be…" Finn actually thinks about it for several moments. "She'll be pleased I've decided to settle down. She thinks it's time I stopped going out and fucking around."

"You've certainly done that."

"Yeah. I guess so."

"Any thoughts on the guest list?"

Finn shakes his head. "We'll have to walk the line on that one. Meet people's expectations for what a Hughes wedding should be without the damn thing getting out of control."

"And what about your Dad?"

He blinks, like I'm the one who's gone too far. Finn has no idea. Anger burns in the middle of my chest. Anger that hardly seems to belong to me. I don't get pissed and have outbursts. That's never been a tool in my arsenal. I don't know that I've ever been angry like this.

"What about my Dad?"

"Will he be able to attend the ceremony? If he's going to, we'll have to design it around his abilities. And the reception..." I purse my lips and stare at a spot above Finn's head. "Daphne and Emerson barely got away with five hundred people at the reception. A Hughes wedding, though...that's seven-fifty minimum."

"Eva, this—"

"You'll have to make some decisions if you're going to get the outcome you want. You know better than I do what your Dad is capable of. I have the feeling it's one thing or another. Either he'll be able to attend the ceremony, or he'll be able to make a speech at the reception."

"There's time to figure that out."

"Did you like the food tonight?"

Finn's eyes narrow. "I didn't eat."

"Oh, right. You came late. Is the catering something you wanted me to handle?"

He's silent for a moment that hangs and

drags. It twists itself together with the pain in my heart. "You don't have to handle any of it. We can get married at the courthouse, for all I care."

I laugh like he's made a real joke. "A courthouse wouldn't be nearly enough for the press releases. Be serious, Finn."

"I *am* serious. We can decide all of this later."

"That's just not how events like this go. It's possible to throw together a wedding in a short period of time, but not ideal. And it's not like when Leo and Haley got married. You're Finn Hughes, remember?"

"For now," he shoots back. "And it's a wedding, not a trade negotiation. It can be as simple as getting a license."

"You've got it all figured out, then." *This* is what he's decided, all by himself. A fake date is one thing. A fake relationship. A fake engagement, even. But a fake marriage? One that has no real love in it, only duty?

That's what Finn is offering. He's going to put a ring on my finger and push me away. He'll keep me in a separate wing of his house, in a separate wing of his *life,* and hold me at arm's length while he waits for the future he thinks is inevitable.

That's not what I want from Finn. I might've

told myself that, but I don't want something fake. That's never what I wanted, even when I knew it would hurt.

"Eva." *He* sounds hurt now, and it's bullshit. I'm not the one who hurt him. He hurt me. He stood here in this art gallery and did it again and again. "It'll be easier once we're married."

"There's just one problem." I draw myself up to my full height and cross my arms over my chest. I'm not just protecting myself. I'm protecting a little piece of Finn, too.

It gives me a warm, glowing feeling to think of protecting our child, even when I'm mad as hell because Finn is doing this to me now. Standing here like what we had didn't matter. Standing here like he can offer me a hollow imitation of a marriage and have that be enough.

"What's that?" Finn asks. His eyes go dark, like he's replaying our conversation to find some detail he missed.

"You never asked me to marry you." His eyes widen. "You never asked. And I will never, ever say yes."

I turn my back on him and walk away.

CHAPTER SIX

Finn

I AM A fool in every possible way.

I'm a fool for going to that wedding reception instead of just going to Eva's apartment and begging for forgiveness. I'm a fool for announcing to her that we'd get married. As if Eva Morelli, a queen, would agree to my pathetic offer. *No one tells Leo Morelli what to do,* she said to me, once upon a time. Well, nobody tells Eva Morelli what to do, either.

At least they don't stare at a painting and announce she'll marry them.

"You look like you chewed up a lemon." Hemingway leans against the doorway to the den, surveying me with raised eyebrows.

"Thanks."

"That was code for *what made you look like*

you chewed up a lemon, Finn? Bad night out on the town?"

"Yes. I had a horrendous night."

"One of my friends texted me to say that you had a fight with Eva Morelli at her sister's wedding."

My God. It's never going to end, is it?

Oh, it will. Before you want it to. The matter-of-fact voice in my head won't shut the hell up.

"We didn't. We had a discussion."

"Something go wrong with your fake engagement?"

"Jesus, Hem. Keep your voice down."

"Sorry." Now he uses an exaggerated whisper. "I meant, it's clear something went wrong with your fake engagement. Do you want to talk about it?"

I flip the laptop in front of me closed. I've been trying to work since early this morning, when I woke up in a rage at myself. I took a rage-shower, rage-dressed, and I've been rage-working for the better part of two hours.

I don't have the words to tell Hemingway exactly how this went wrong. I'll look like a giant fucking hypocrite. Worse, I have no plan. My plan *was* to marry her. Eva stomped that under her high heel.

"I can't talk about it yet," I admit. "I don't know how to explain it. I'm too pissed off."

He gives me big eyes now. "At her?"

"At myself."

"Well." Hemingway straightens up. "You should call her instead of sitting here looking like that. It'll be better if you're on the same side."

"How do you know we're not?"

"Because of your face."

"Jesus Christ."

"Also, it's time for breakfast. Are you coming?"

"Fine."

There is relative peace in the kitchen. Hemingway gives me a thumbs-up from his seat at the table. Jennifer's sliding eggs onto plates.

"This is just how I like them," my father says. I take a seat on his other side. At least he's having a good morning.

"Finn had a bad night last night," Hemingway announces.

I give him a death glare.

"A bad night?" My dad looks at me over his glasses. "Did you overindulge at one of your parties?"

"Yes, that's exactly it."

In a way, Hemingway is right. I overindulged

in Eva. I touched her and kissed her and fucked her in an art gallery. I said yet another damn-fool thing to her. *And* I didn't follow her when she turned on her heel and left.

"Orange juice," my father says. He reaches out with his fork and taps my glass. "That'll help."

"Will it?"

"It's good for hangovers."

Hemingway grins at me, the little asshole. "That's what I've heard, too. Orange juice is great for hangovers."

"You know what else is great for hangovers? Silence."

Hemingway pretends to zip his lips, then attacks his eggs and toast. The three of us eat in a quiet that could be companionable if I weren't so pissed.

It's seeping out of me and into the rest of them.

It hasn't been more than five minutes when Hemingway stands up and whisks his plate away. "That was great. I have homework. See you later, Dad."

"Let me know if you need me to look it over," Dad says.

"You know I will, Dad." Hemingway smiles

from the kitchen doorway and then he's gone.

My eggs and toast are tasteless. I keep eating them anyway. Jennifer makes herself busy at the sink. I can tell she's taking care to give us privacy while she watches over my dad.

"So." Dad doesn't seem to mind his eggs. Not at all. "Long night, then?"

"Yes."

Normally, I'd tell him a story. Keep him engaged as long as I can. I don't have it in me right now.

He waits. I can feel his eyes on me. "A party got out of hand, is that it?"

I rub a hand over my face. "There wasn't any party, Dad. Hemingway was joking. I just didn't get much sleep."

"Something on your mind?"

"No."

If I'm going to tell him, I want him to understand. I know that's not possible. It pisses me off that the world could be so cruel. It enrages me that I haven't made it any better by existing.

"Sometimes I feel better if I just talk it out."

"There's really nothing to say."

He finishes his toast and leans back in his chair, a glass of orange juice in his hand. "Does it have to do with one of your friends?"

"Does *what* have to do with one of my friends?"

He raises his eyebrows at me, looking so much like Hemingway that my chest clenches. "Your lack of sleep. Your bad night."

"What's on your schedule today, Dad?"

"Phineas."

"Any meetings? Are you going to play golf?"

I'm an asshole. I don't just feel like one. I am the physical embodiment of a fucking prick. I can't help being angry with him, even knowing that it's mostly myself I want to throttle. I can't help wanting more time. I can't help wanting more than I can get.

"I'm not too interested in my schedule. I'm interested in you." He takes a sip of orange juice.

"I'm really fine."

"Finn, as long as I've known you, you've never been so angry at eggs."

"I'm not—" I stab my fork too hard into the scrambled eggs and the tines scrape on the plate. "I'm not angry at the eggs."

He's lucid for now, but time is short. It's short for everything. Short to figure out what to do with Eva. Short to figure out how to protect the child from something I can't protect it from.

It's short, but it's so goddamn long. She's

going to have to spend years without me. Or worse, years caring for me *and* a child.

I don't want that for Eva. If she has a son—if she has *my* son—then that's it. That's the rest of her life. Gone with a snap of my fingers.

If I wasn't here, then none of it would have happened. It goes far beyond asking her on a date with me at the Morelli Mansion. We'd have to go back years to stop all this.

"Tell me what's bothering you."

I breathe out some of the fiery hurt in my chest. Toss the fork onto the tablecloth. My dad's looking at me, his expression calm. I hate it. I hate that these moments with him are all we have left. He won't even remember it. There's no point in asking the question. There's no point in having this conversation at all.

"Why?" So much for not asking. "Why did you even *have* children if you knew how it would end?"

He blinks at me.

I've gone too far. Asked him a question that's beyond him to answer. And anyway, it's too late. Hemingway and I are here, like it or not. I open my mouth to take it back, but I'm too choked up. By everything. By the fact that a baby is going to be born who has to suffer what I suffered. By the fact that my own father might not know what the hell I'm talking about.

"Well, Finn." He sets his orange juice on the tablecloth and drums his fingertips next to it. "Children are a sign of hope."

"Even if it's hopeless?"

He shrugs. There's a flash of confusion in his eyes. I don't know if it means he's lost track of the conversation or if he just doesn't understand where I'm coming from.

But then…

"I would make the argument that nothing's ever hopeless so long as we're alive."

"No? What if it's our destiny to lose everything? That seems hopeless."

"Oh, come now. Destiny is about hope, too."

"And what if it's not? What if your destiny is hopelessness? What if you know you can't change anything?"

"That can't be." A twinkle comes to his eyes. "You can't know the ending until you've reached it. A person's fate can change any time."

"I'm talking about kids, Dad. About having children even in the face of a future you don't want."

"Do you have proof?"

"Of the future?"

Yes. He's sitting right in front of me. I can't avoid becoming him. In less than a decade, I'll be headed firmly down that path. I don't say that out loud.

"Aha. You *don't*. Because you can't. Nobody knows what the future will bring."

"Didn't you?"

"Of course not. I had no idea how wonderful you'd be." He laughs, and I can't take it. I can't. The wash of feeling. The way my mind ticks off his genuine laughter. I won't hear it many more times. "I know quite a bit about business. Not so much about children. I was terrified when I learned you were on your way."

"That I wouldn't be what you expected?"

"That I wouldn't be what you needed." He purses his lips. "I stand by what I said. Children are about hope. Hope that the future will be worthy of them, of course. But the hope that they'll forgive you your mistakes. And you'll learn to rise to the occasion. You're a step ahead of me."

"How's that?"

"You've always been pragmatic, Phineas. You know we're all the same, in the end."

"Are we?"

"Everybody is born." He traces a line on the tablecloth. "Everyone dies one day."

"How is that hopeful?"

"It's hopeful because everything happens while you're alive. You've always known you'd only be here a little while. Always understood that." He lifts his hands in front of him and makes two fists. "You've always taken life by the throat because of it."

"Are you sure I wasn't just a hopeless asshole?"

"Look. Life is between you and God. A deal's not done until both parties have signed on the dotted line. It's not over until it's over. There's always hope."

Maybe he's right. Maybe I've always known too much. Maybe I've denied myself hope because I was so bent on certainty.

I told myself I was taking as much as I could from life, but none of it was what I wanted. All those people, all those hookups, all those parties—I didn't want any of them. They were only cheap, shallow replacements for what I really want.

Eva. Always Eva.

She's beautiful and strong and so fucking competent she makes lesser men weep. Most of them couldn't handle her. They don't like someone smarter than them. I'm not afraid of it.

It makes me want her even more.

"I like this toast," he says.

"What?"

"The toast. It's good." Dad looks me in the eye, and I laugh. This is the kind of absurd thing he used to say when I was upset about something as a child. When I thought something was the end of the world. Before I understood that the end of the world was already happening. "But you know what, Phineas?"

"Tell me."

"It's better with more butter and jam. You can swear up and down that you love toast even if it's just dry bread, but that's just denying the truth. It's better with jam. Speaking of—" He takes a spoon from a small dish at the center of the table and puts jam on his remaining piece of toast. "There. It's better. Where do we get this jam, anyway? It's the best I've tasted."

"Jennifer makes it at home, actually." It's one of her hobbies. A jar appears in the fridge every couple of weeks. Blackberry. Raspberry. A particularly piquant gooseberry.

"Now." My dad takes a bite, and his eyes flutter closed. "Something was bothering you. Are you going to tell me what it is?"

CHAPTER SEVEN

Eva

N OW THAT THE news is out to Finn, there's
nothing to do but throw myself into work.

Am I avoiding the problem? Absolutely not.
There is no problem. Finn's idea of an acceptable
solution is to get real-married and live sad,
separate lives. He won't even think about the
baby.

The end.

There is not another person on earth I can
talk to about this. Not yet. I didn't want to tell
any of my family before I told Finn. Leo doesn't
even know.

It feels wrong. I don't like having to walk
around with this secret all to myself. But I don't
want to give them this story, either. That Finn
offered to make the engagement real, to actually

marry me, and I turned him down.

I can picture my mother's polite, horrified expression. I can picture Leo's fury. Daphne's concern. Sophia's raised eyebrows.

And then…what?

A notification pops up on my screen.

Apparently I've been invited to a meeting with a possible donor. A last-minute meeting. Five minutes from now, at the end of the day.

These meetings happen semi-frequently. Our family is the primary donor to the Morelli Fund, but we occasionally have other benefactors. Wealthy friends of the family or business partners of my father or my brothers. We've had a few wealthy recluses approach us who have a specific project in mind but need someone to steward it.

It's a funny quirk of my job that it takes so much work to give away money. You can't just throw it at people, otherwise it goes to waste.

I accept the meeting.

What else am I going to do, anyway? I could go visit Leo and Haley. I could have dinner with Daphne and Emerson. I could even text Sophia.

But it's getting harder and harder to stop myself from telling them. Or from giving myself away.

I'm not making any big announcements to

anyone in the family before we can all be reassured of a plan moving forward. They won't be reassured by the fact that I'm keeping the baby.

I can handle the details of caring for my child. I have no doubt about that. As for handling the fallout of a broken heart…

They're not going to be convinced. I'm just not capable of sustaining the fiction of a happy marriage for the rest of my life if none of it is real.

Also, I have to break it to Leo in a way that convinces him not to murder Finn.

I stand up from my desk and stretch. This isn't exactly how I'd like to feel before a meeting with a possible donor. It's almost six o'clock. My makeup has worn off. My shirt is rumpled, somehow.

Maybe I should have gone into the offices at Morelli Holdings. I've spent a lot of time making my office at home beautiful and comfortable over the years. Now it feels closed, almost oppressive. Every piece in this room was chosen by a woman who was heartbroken, yes, but who didn't think the situation would get any worse. She did not think the situation would be complicated by the arrival of Finn Hughes.

She was wrong.

My secretary steps into the room. Ryan has

been with me for two years. He's very competent. I'm accidentally scowling at him when he enters the room. "Ms. Morelli, the donor is here—are you sure you want to go ahead with the meeting?"

I rearrange my face into a socially acceptable expression. "Yes. Send them in please."

"Okay." He steps out of my office, reappearing a moment later with someone else.

With *Finn,* following close behind him.

I am...dumbfounded. Ryan doesn't know what to do with that. He looks between me and Finn.

"We're good for the day, Ryan," I say. "You can head out for the evening. I'll see you tomorrow."

Finn steps back to let Ryan leave. Then he bustles into my office and puts a binder in the center of the desk, like he's setting up for a pitch meeting.

"What the hell are you doing?"

Finn extends his hand to me. "Finn Hughes. I'm here to discuss a potential donation to the Morelli Fund."

I shake his hand because this is so bizarre and so *wrong.* "I'd like to discuss you leaving my office. Immediately."

Finn sits. He looks up at me, eyes wide with

hope and resignation, until I sit, too.

"Before I go, there's a particular project I want the Morelli Fund to work on."

"Again, I don't see how—"

"It's for the Dementia Foundation."

Oh God. Here I was, all set to be steely and unforgiving. But with Finn's hazel eyes looking into mine with despair covered in a thin layer of hope, I can't quite follow through on kicking him out.

I'll have to get used to it eventually.

I fold my hands on the desk. "You're fully capable of starting and funding your own foundation."

Finn flips past the first few pages of his hard-copy presentation and holds the cover open. There, in plain, printed text, is the proposed structure of the project as directed by the Morelli Fund.

He glances at it, then back at me. "I don't want my own foundation."

His voice is so low, and so rough with regret, that I make fists under the desk instead of reaching for him. My hurt and anger are like a knot around my heart. The longing, though? That's worse. It's a thousand extra pebbles spilled into one of my terrariums. The balance is all off.

And I can see that longing reflected in Finn's eyes. His hand flexes on the desk, his fist closing tight and opening again.

"Have you seen a doctor?" he asks.

"The baby is none of your concern. Neither is my pregnancy. That's what happens when you tell someone they were a *good time,* but it's over."

His mouth tightens. This is not part of his pitch. Not even in the realm of what we're supposed to be discussing. But it's been so heavy to keep this to myself. To just…wake up with it every day. Go to sleep with it every night.

All I want him to say is that he wants this baby with me. I know it's impossible.

Finn's hand flexes on his pitch binder. "Your pregnancy is a concern to me, Eva. And so are you."

"I can handle making an appointment."

"But you haven't made one yet?"

"No," I admit.

Finn glances at the presentation, then back at me. He's the acting CEO of Hughes Industries. He knows better than to derail philanthropic meetings with personal, emotional bullshit. "When did you find out?"

"An hour after you broke up with me."

He blows out a breath. "I'm sorry."

"It's none of your business."

"Eva."

"Oh—did you want more details? Here's how it went, Finn. I took twenty-four pregnancy tests and then shut down emotionally. I'm still in denial. And I'm still pissed at you."

"I'm sorry." The corners of Finn's mouth turn down. The skin around his eyes is tight. He means this apology. "That I made you feel like you were alone. This child is our responsibility. Together."

Ugh. That's the thing. I don't want to be his responsibility. I want to be *more*.

A bolt of understanding shoots through me.

This is why Sophia gets so frustrated with me for never needing her. For insisting on this one-sided duty, where I give, and nobody can give back to me. It's a strangely fresh perspective. I've never allowed myself to be on the other side. Now that Finn's turned it on me…

"Seriously, Finn. Why are you here? To ask me about a doctor? I'll see a doctor. Don't worry about it."

"I *am* worried about it. Also, I wanted to ask you to reconsider my proposal."

It didn't take him long, did it? I'm pissed again. My expression drops into a Morelli glare.

Not appropriate for a potential donor meeting, but if *this* is what he has to say?

"There was no proposal. There was an edict from King Hughes."

He takes his hand from the proposal deck. "Do you want me to ask?"

"That's beside the fact that I would say no."

Another shadow across the hazel of his eyes. "Do you want me to *beg*?"

It wouldn't hurt. "No. I want you to leave."

Finn glares back at me. "Do you want me to get on one knee in front of everyone in Bishop's Landing?"

"Now you're just mocking me." Also, yes. Yes, I want that very much. I've never wanted it with anyone else, but I want everyone to know he loves me. I don't want some bullshit fake proposal. I want the real thing, and I want everyone to see it.

He sighs. "You know that getting married is what's best for the child."

"Why?" I fire the question at him like a demand. It *is* a demand. "So he can have a father, or so he can join the Hughes cult of secrets? I'm not doing that. I'm not raising a child in a home where he knows he's not wanted."

Finn scowls, leaning back an inch like he can make this less painful if there's more space between us. He looks young and pissed and passionate. And he looks tired beyond his years.

He doesn't say a word. He doesn't refute the argument that he doesn't want this baby. I don't even expect him to.

I sit up straight. Regain control. "I need time to think."

"No."

"You need to respect my boundaries, Finn. If there's any chance of us working this out, you have to."

"Do you want to work it out?"

"Honestly? I don't know. We might both be better off going our separate ways."

He closes the cover of the presentation and stands. "I'm leaving this pitch deck here for you to read. Please get in touch when you're finished. I'd like to talk to you about it."

There's so much more he wants to say. It's written all over his face and in every tense line of his body.

Is he searching for the right words, too? Part of me wants to tell him there's nothing he can do to make it up to me. And part of me wants to call off this argument right now.

I don't want to marry you out of obligation. If you think of me that way, I can't. If you think of the baby that way, I can't. I know you're afraid. I know you didn't think of me as a duty before. Don't start now. Please.

None of it is prepared half as well as his pitch deck or even my first attempts at a decent terrarium. The words are a clump of broken cacti and ferns that don't match. I can't hand him my broken heart and say *here, look. Doesn't it make sense? Ask me to marry you like you love me. I know you love me. I thought you loved me.*

It's not getting any better. I have the distinct sense that I'm running out of time.

Finn looks at me for another long moment. It's painful at my very core to be on the opposite side of the desk from him. To be on opposite sides of this argument. We should be on the same team. If nothing else, we should be facing this together.

What do I have to do? Get naked? Take him to bed? How do we solve this?

How do I let *him* solve this?

He takes one step away from my desk, and I have the urge to chase him. To shout after him. Even to scream. That's how much I want him to stay. I'm the one who told him I wouldn't abandon him. I said it without condition. I meant it.

But I know better than to give in to that feeling. I know better than to let myself be beholden to it.

I've made that mistake before, and I'm not going to do it again.

"Finn," I call.

It's too late. He doesn't come back.

Chapter Eight

Eva

WHEN MY APARTMENT is empty for the evening, I stride out of my office like a high-powered CEO leaving her Manhattan high rise and proceed directly to the bathroom to run a bath.

There's conflicting evidence about how much caffeine is too much to have when you're pregnant, but I don't want to take the risk. Even though my craving for Diet Coke has reached monstrous proportions. I can't have wine, either, but I need something to take the edge off the pitch deck.

That's how I end up with a can of sparkling blackberry water.

I take an ice-cold can with me when the bath is finished running. A small shelf at the side of my soaking tub has a circular indentation for drinks.

The warm water feels good. I don't turn it to scalding like I usually do—I read it's not good for the baby. It's strange how much being pregnant affects everything. And nothing. I'm expected to go about my day like normal. Meanwhile, everything's changing. I'm tired in strange ways. My stomach feels nauseous one minute and ravenous the next. I'm exhausted, and then five minutes later I can't imagine sleeping.

Floating in the tub with the icy metal of the can in my palm helps.

I'm not going to look at the pitch deck to-night.

I move it to the corner of my desk the next morning. No in-person meetings on my schedule for today. Paperwork. Emails. I studiously ignore the pitch deck.

At five, I leave the office. I take the pitch with me, though.

If I'm going to read it, it's going to be on my own time. Not because Finn tries to hijack my position at the Morelli Fund to get an in.

I change out of the outfit I wore to work. Wash my face. Pat it dry.

Then I take the pitch to a sitting room that now doubles as a work room.

This is where I keep all my supplies for making terrariums. I don't use a typical craft shelf to store them. The jars of materials are in a one-of-a-kind piece in the shape of an octagon. Irregular shelves make a pattern that seems more intentional the farther away you stand.

I start on a new terrarium.

New bowl. New layer of pebbles. New dirt.

I'm picturing something simple, but beautiful. I've done a sunken ship, a lighthouse, a castle. This one is going to feature a fairy house carved out of a mushroom.

It's cute and whimsical. It might seem silly to some people, but I think life needs a little whimsy.

The pitch deck waits for me, patient but stalwart. Unrelenting.

It's a formal business deck with black plastic binding and a clear cover.

"What's the purpose of you?" I ask the deck conversationally. "Why not just send me an email? Or better yet, why not just tell me what he's thinking? What's the point of a deck?"

I work on the terrarium, pressing down the bottom layer with my fingertips. Working a tiny cactus into a spot near the center. Its flower hasn't bloomed yet. It's hiding in a furl of pale green, but I know it's there. In a week there will be bright pink petals, their silkiness a contrast to the cactus's spikes.

"How long do I put off reading you, hmm? A day? A week?"

The pitch deck doesn't answer.

The silence seems more and more accusatory.

It's been another twenty minutes when I finish with the first phase of the terrarium, straighten up from the worktable, and brush off my hands.

Fine. I'll read it. But only because I'm good and ready. Not because I'm on fire with curiosity. Not because it's burning my lungs. I angle the lamp at the corner of the table, slide the terrarium out of the way, and pull the deck in front of me.

"Let's see what's here."

The cover opens to reveal the title page. Neat. A clear font. A simple title.

Hughes-Morelli Joint Venture.

My throat closes. I clear it and turn to the next page, tipping it so I can read.

It's a proposal. An *actual* proposal.

Proposal, reads the top header.

And under that:

A Proposal by Phineas Hughes to Eva Morelli, regarding the contract of marriage.

There's a paragraph of text making it explicitly clear that the proposal is meant as a supplementary document to provide context to the larger question at hand.

The first sub-heading reads: *Advantages.*

Then there's a bulleted list.

ATTRACTION: According to societal standards of beauty, he's at least an eight. Maybe even a nine when it's gray sweatpants season. And he promises to give you two orgasms for every one of his.

NETWORK: A relationship via marriage with him will include access to a wide range of social connections that would benefit the Morelli Fund and family.

COMMITMENT: He has years of experience managing family commitments and relationships. Colloquially, this is known as being "ride or die."

I burst out laughing, which immediately turns into a sob.

This is Finn, baring himself on literal paper.

The fourth bullet point:

FAMILY: Son of Geneva Roosevelt and

Daniel Hughes. Good parents, both still living. One brother, Hemingway Hughes—a captivating conversationalist, if a bit of a rascal.

CONNECTION: Deep interest in Eva Morelli. Companionship would be mutually beneficial.

Please continue reading for a discussion of risks.

It's an interesting choice, because a risk isn't the opposite of an advantage. It's not a weakness or a failing. It's something that might go wrong in some future, hypothetical space.

A risk might not happen.

GENETICS: Genetic condition has a significant impact on both parties in a Hughes marriage.

PLAYBOY: His number is high, so to speak. This didn't seem to be a dealbreaker before.

DANGER: Prone to adrenaline-seeking behaviors. Colloquially known as YOLO.

I laugh again. Hot tears run down my cheeks.

I can hear his wry tone as if he were in the room.

ATTACHMENT: He cares about you too much. It's a problem.

Holding back my tears is a fool's errand. I've been crying a lot more lately. Between that and the morning sickness, I'm a completely different person. A watering pot, basically. My emotions are more intense than they've ever been. Is that because I'm pregnant? Or is that because I'm in love?

Part of me wants to call Finn right now and accept the proposal… though I'm not sure a pitch deck can really count as a marriage proposal, can it? Even if he doesn't love me, he can be kind. We'll have this child together either way. Maybe marriage to him *is* the best option.

The problem is that I wouldn't stop loving him.

It would break my heart to live with that distance between us every single day. I can't keep battering myself against it. His will is too strong. I'll wind up broken, the way I was after Lane.

It felt so real, like I was in love. Only later did I wonder why I'd thought I could love a man so much older than me. What did we have in common? Those logical questions didn't bother me at the time. My nineteen-year-old self was willing to believe in an unlikely fairy tale.

Then, when I told Leo about my feelings for Lane, he confessed.

He confessed that it was Caroline who'd hurt him, and that his physical injuries hadn't been the worst of it. That he believed it was the only reason Lane pursued me. By then, Lane had fallen for me. He didn't accept the breakup easily. But by then I saw who he really was. I saw who I really was—a pawn in the game of an older man.

I cried every day for a month. I swore I'd never be so broken again.

Through my tears, I read the next part of Finn's proposal.

I accept your decision regarding the issue of marriage. A partnership only makes sense if both parties benefit. If you feel the advantages outweigh the risks, then I would be honored to become your husband.

How am I supposed to live with this proposal in my head? How am I supposed to walk around every day knowing that Finn sat down and assessed himself with clear eyes? He offered himself to me in this business-deal format because he knew it would make me laugh. And maybe it was the only way for him to present it to me calmly, without breaking down.

I might break down, too, if I knew I only had seven years left.

Which probably explains the final section—the joint project with the Morelli Fund, benefiting the Dementia Foundation. It involves researching new treatments and preventative strategies.

> *Such medical innovations may help future generations of Hughes. It's unlikely that even with help, doctors would find a cure in this generation. Basing a life around the possibility of a cure would be indulging in false hope.*

I flip the cover of the proposal closed.

That's how he thinks about hope. That it's false. "You don't know that for sure."

That's the argument. He wants all of our choices to be based on the worst-case scenario. I can see the wisdom in that kind of planning for lots of situations.

Not this one.

It would make a wedding feel like a funeral. It would turn every dream into a cruel joke.

I won't participate in making a joke out of

Finn Hughes. I won't help him lead a sham life while his heart breaks more with every day that passes.

The baby won't understand Finn's emotional distance. The baby won't know that it comes from fear and grief and guilt. Can he overcome those things for our child?

Can he overcome them for me?

"Nobody knows what's going to happen." I'm stern with the proposal the way I should have been stern with Finn before. "You can't make me accept the worst before it's here. I won't do it. I want to be *happy* with you, goddamn it. This baby deserves to be happy. And loved."

I pick up my phone, thumbs flying over the screen before I can stop myself.

Eva: *I've reviewed your proposal.*
Finn: *And?*
Eva: *You need to get some things straight.*
Finn: *Like what?*

Like the fact that I'm in love with you. Like the fact that I want to drag you into a happy ending, despite your best efforts to end in tragedy. Like the fact that you're breaking my heart.

My phone rings in my hand.

"What do I need to get straight?" Finn's voice

is guarded. Careful. He sounds as tired as I feel. As heartsick as I feel. And still hopeful, despite what he wrote in the letter.

He doesn't want to create false hope.

It's too late. I have every kind of hope, even the false kind.

"Maybe I don't have time to discuss it," I say, stalling for time.

"Humor me."

Humoring Finn Hughes means buying into the idea that he is doomed, the idea that we're both doomed. The idea that our child is doomed. It's a cornerstone of his proposal, in fact. One of his *risks.* He has a limited amount of time, and I don't want to believe that.

I've always been the levelheaded one. I'm the daughter who handles things. Love isn't something that can be handled. It can't be boxed off until it fits neatly in the guest wing of the Hughes estate.

His words come back to me.

It's for the Dementia Foundation.

Finn's not just clarifying his personal proposal in this pitch deck. He's suggesting we work together to change things for the child. Even that strikes me as fatalistic. *It's too late for him.*

How would I manage this project, this sadness, without any hope for the man I love?

"It's a great proposal. Perfect. But you're missing the point. You don't want the baby."

"That's not the important point."

"That's the *only* point."

The phone rings again. Since I'm already on a call with Finn, it's just an incessant beeping. I pull it away from my face. Leo's name is on the screen. Relief fills me, because I don't want to talk to Finn right now. I can't. And you know what? He doesn't deserve an answer right away. If he had gotten down on one knee, then I would have answered him right away. Instead he presented me with a pitch deck. So maybe I'll respond the same way, with a memo on corporate letterhead.

"My brother's calling. I have to go."

"Eva, wait—"

I hang up. Finn can wait until I'm good and ready. I swipe at my eyes and clear my throat while the call connects. I don't want Leo to know I was crying. "Hey. What's—"

"It's happening." Leo's voice is shaking. Terse chatter rises in the background. A car door slams. "Haley's in labor. You have to come. I need you."

CHAPTER NINE

Eva

GETTING TO THE hospital involves a flurry of activity.

I summon my driver and notify my security team. The oversized silk blouse and shorts I wore for working on a terrarium won't work. I quickly change into black slacks, structured but comfortable. A black sleeveless top. And a sweater, tucked over the top of my purse.

I'm not sure how long I'll be there. I can almost guarantee that I'll need to step in at some point. If I do—*when* I do—I'll look every inch the intimidating Morelli princess.

It's too early for Haley to be in labor by several weeks.

The date gives me a sick feeling in my stomach, but I push it away.

Babies come early all the time. There is no need to panic. And even if there *was* a need, I can't. Not right now. My brother needs me. My sister-in-law needs me. My little niece needs me. I call ahead to the hospital to tell them I'm on my way. A pleasant-sounding woman answers the phone. I let her know that my brother and his wife will be arriving shortly.

It's a courtesy. Leo can be disruptive at the best of times. From the way he sounded on the phone, it's not the best of times.

It's certain to be very tense at the hospital.

It could even be an emergency.

Eva: *I'm on my way.*

Leo: *Ten minutes.*

The plan has been in place since early on in Haley's pregnancy. Of course, everyone's top priority is keeping her and the baby safe and happy. The fact that it's all being set into motion earlier than expected won't change that.

It will, however, change things for Leo.

There are reasons I've been his emergency contact for more than half our lives. Reasons why there's paperwork on file at every local hospital giving permission for me to be with him regardless of any policies for visitors and visiting hours.

One of those reasons is that my brother, the infamous Beast of Bishop's Landing, has the worst white-coat syndrome of anyone on earth.

His blood pressure skyrockets at the sight of a medical building. I've sat in many, many appointments with him, watching him get more and more snappish and unreasonable. Then, once we've walked out: *I couldn't hear a damn thing they said. My heart was pounding in my ears.*

Finn: I hope everything's okay.

I know I should shut him out. Keep him at arm's length. But I'm too focused on staying calm to do it.

Eva: Haley's gone into labor. It's early and seems sudden, so I'm not sure if there will be complications. I'm arriving at the hospital now.

Finn: Is there anything you need?

For you to understand that I love you. For you to understand that you can't freeze out our baby. I won't even give you the chance.

I don't get the chance to send a response. My driver pulls up at the hospital's emergency entrance and another text arrives.

Leo: They took her away.

Shit.

My driver hands off the keys to the valet and comes with me into the building. A nurse is waiting to take us to the OB wing. Two of Leo's people are waiting outside the doors wearing grim expressions.

I go through and find two more nurses speaking in hushed tones at the nurses' station, stealing glances at a door across the way.

Not a great sign.

When my brother is most afraid, he doubles down on being in control. I'm not sure it's a winning strategy at the moment.

I follow the sound of his voice to a room marked *TRIAGE* and find Leo arguing with a nurse, his face pale. He's standing up too tall and too tense. Half a step, and he'd be looming over her.

"—understand. This wasn't the plan. How long are you going to keep me from my wife?"

"It depends on the procedure to—"

"How long *exactly*?"

"Leo." I step into the room and go to his side, giving the nurse a small smile. A line appears on her forehead. I'd be wary if I were her, too. "My name is Eva. I'll be staying as a support person. What's the situation with Haley?"

"Tell her," barks Leo.

The nurse doesn't flinch. "Haley is being prepped for a C-section. It is urgent, but she'll be able to be awake during the procedure. No one can enter the operating room until her spinal block has been placed."

No wonder he can't hear. They wheeled his heart into another room and are currently putting a needle into her spine.

Leo's vibrating with fury. That's what it looks like to everyone else, anyway. But his fear has always looked like anger. He cultivated that idea on purpose.

It works on other people. Not so much on me.

"What are the next steps?" I ask the nurse, a hand on his elbow. If he's going to completely lose his shit, it's best that nobody else is in the room.

"You'll wait here until I come back with scrubs. When it's time, I'll escort you to the operating room."

Leo glares at her until she's gone, his dark eyes murderous.

I rub at his arm. "You have to calm down."

"This is because of me." He looks down at me, the nurse forgotten, a terrified red spreading across his cheeks. "I made this happen."

"Leo. What?"

"I had a dream last night that something went wrong with the baby. With her cord. And when we got here, they took one look at that monitor and said the fucking thing might be wrapped around her neck. Then they took both of them. What if this was because of me?"

"It wasn't you," I soothe. "It was just a—a coincidental dream. Don't think about it anymore. We're just going to wait for the nurse to bring the scrubs, and I'll walk down there with you. How's Haley?"

"I don't know. I can't see her." He grits his teeth. "I barely had time to talk to her."

"The doctors here are good. Remember? You interviewed most of them. You can trust these people."

"The way you could trust Finn?" He's scowling now, eyes narrowed and dark. I know that look. He's hunting for a problem he can solve. By force, if necessary.

"We don't need to talk about Finn right now."

"Yes, we do." He's insistent, tone sharp. "You're sad. You've been sad for days. What did that motherfucker do to you?"

"Nothing."

He paces away, stabbing a finger in my direction. "Don't lie to me. He hurt you. I want to know what he did. I want to know why you've been so goddamn sad. Don't bother pretending you're not."

"Jesus. I'm thirty-three. Calm down."

Leo laughs, and the sound tells me exactly how hard he's spiraling. He's basically unhinged from fear. "No, I don't think I will. I think I'll kill him like I should have killed Lane."

"*Leo*." It's ice water and adrenaline to hear him say that. The words dredge up old memories filtered through shock and pain. I'm not aware of crossing the room to him. Only that I've taken his face in my hands and given him a desperate shake. It's over the top. I don't care. The thought scares me to death. "Don't say that."

His teeth scrape together. Leo's been taller than me and stronger than me for years, but right now, he's on the verge of breaking down. Fixating on revenge is the only way he can think to regain control. It's a fire lighting in his eyes behind a sheen of furious tears.

But he can't say that. Not here.

Because after Lane Constantine died, the cops learned I'd had an affair with him. That made me a suspect. Leo's reputation as my ultra-protective, violent brother made him one, too. We were both questioned.

Neither of us had alibis for that night. Secretly, I've always suspected that Leo might have been the one to murder Lane. Sometimes, I think he secretly suspects me.

In the end, it doesn't matter if one of us was the killer. I would never let him go to prison for Lane's death, and he would never let that happen to me.

Still, the past is in the room with us now. Again. And if I lose his attention, if he goes down that path, he'll lose it.

"You're holding your breath." I don't think he knows. "You'd feel better if you let it out."

"That fucker," he says, his voice rough, "messed you up for life."

"I'm not messed up."

He widens his eyes, and from this close, I can see the accusation there. His worry. His fear. Those memories feel like a crowd in this silly triage room with Haley's hospital bag abandoned on the floor. New memories pile on. All of them include Finn.

"Well, I went and broke my own rule." I meant to sound defiant and dismissive, but my voice breaks instead. "I fell in love, and—"

The first sob catches me off guard.

Leo curses under his breath and breaks my grip on his face. Then he folds his arms around me. He runs one palm up and down my back. "He wasn't worthy of you, sister mine. No man is. We're fucking barbarians. All of us."

I'm overwhelmed by sadness and longing and missing Finn, but at least Leo is calmer now. This is how it works. Only one of us can freak out at a time.

Finn apologized for making me feel alone, but I don't have to be.

"I need you to know something," I say into his shirt. "This is, like, *not* the best time to tell you. I realize that. But—"

"I already know he broke your heart."

"Yeah. The thing is, I'm pregnant."

Leo's hands go to my shoulders. He pushes me back a little so he can get a clear view of my face. I'm a mess. Hot tears. A runny nose. Every inch a Morelli princess. "What?"

"I'm pregnant. With Finn's baby. So it's worse than him breaking my heart. And you really can't kill him, Leo. You can't even joke about it."

"You're pregnant." To my shock, Leo's entire face lights up. "You're going to have the baby?"

I can't help but smile back, even while I'm still sobbing. "Yeah."

"Christ, Eva, that's great news. That's what you've always wanted."

"I never told you I wanted a baby."

He crushes me to him again. "Do you think you had to tell me? You think I haven't known you all my life?"

"Finn *broke up* with me. And then he proposed. And we're still fake-engaged. It's a fucking disaster."

"We'll figure it out."

"You *cannot* kill him."

"I won't kill him. Not unless he fucks up again."

"There are a lot of other people to be worried about. Mom and Dad are going to lose their minds unless I can solve this. And Finn—" I can't begin to explain the whole situation with Finn right now. And frankly, I shouldn't. I only wanted to calm Leo down, not do a full debriefing on Finn Hughes. "Things are *really* complicated with Finn."

I don't blame Finn for how complicated it is. Not really. I wish he'd see things from my perspective, but his fears are valid.

"It'll be okay. I promise." The nurse re-enters

the room, and Leo's face pales. "I promise," he says again.

My heart breaks. I wipe my tears and compose myself. *I promise,* even while his wife is in surgery and his baby is coming early and no one on earth can ever guarantee that things will turn out.

The nurse hands over the scrubs. I take Leo's overshirt and give him each piece one by one. His hands are shaking too badly to pull on the surgical cap, so I do it for him.

"She's ready," the nurse says. "Come this way."

I pick up Haley's bag from the floor, tuck Leo's shirt into it, and jog to catch up with them.

"What's the situation inside the OR?" Somebody has to ask the question. That person is me. Leo can't go in blind.

"Haley's had the spinal block. It went well. She's comfortable, and the surgical team is just waiting for the father to get started."

The nurse turns a corner. Another one. There are more stark white walls back here. Fewer neutrals.

She stops in front of a doorway marked *OPERATING ROOM. STERILE ENVIRONMENT.* "Ready?"

Leo looks at me, steeling himself. "It'll be okay?"

This time, he's asking.

"I promise." I mean it for both of us. If everything else goes to hell, we'll find a way out again. "I'll be here when you get back."

CHAPTER TEN

Finn

T HE WOMAN BEHIND the reception desk at the emergency department looks at me with undisguised skepticism. She has brown hair in a large poof and scrubs with Smurfs on them. Those things might have made her seem approachable, but the tiredness in her eyes said she'd worked a long shift. And the hard set of her mouth made it clear she had no interest in who I am.

"Sir, I can't allow unapproved visitors into the emergency department. Or into the OB wing. It's a question of privacy. And security. I'm sure you understand—"

"Finn."

She blinks. "Excuse me?"

"My name is Finn Hughes, but you can call

me Finn."

I see the flash of recognition in her eyes. "Mr. Hughes...Finn...I can't even confirm that Mrs. Morelli is a patient here. It's not that I don't want to help you, but there are rules."

It takes effort to force the patented Finn Hughes charm. "Listen, I know she's a patient here. I'm a friend of the family. A close friend of the family. And I won't go past the waiting room."

"Mr. Hughes, I'm so sorry—" She falls silent as I take out my phone, tap a few things on the screen, and scroll. Then I turn it towards her. "What is that?"

"Twenty million dollars, last year alone."

"What?"

"That's how much Hughes Industries donated to this hospital. Which means I'm invested in the longevity of this healthcare facility. As a major donor, I'd like to tour the waiting room."

Her shoulders stiffen. "A tour can be scheduled at a later time, if—"

"I want to tour it now. Send security with me, if you want. I know these are the Morellis' people."

There are four armed guards in the waiting area of the emergency department. It seemed like the fastest way to get to Eva. Now I'm being stonewalled by a very competent nurse. Normally I would respect that, but nothing about this is normal. My future family is at stake.

"Sir. Mr. Hughes. I cannot just—"

"When I have the new OB wing built, I'll name it after you." I squint at her nametag. "*Cathy*. The Cathy Rosel Obstetrics Wing." A flush darkens her cheeks. "The hospital won't pay a dime. I'm not trying to cause any trouble, I swear. I'm a friend of the family."

A heavy silence.

Then: "You need to follow the signs to the OB department. Do *not* go past the family waiting area, Mr. Hughes. If you do, I'll have you escorted out by security."

I grace her with my best Finn Hughes smile. "The Cathy Rosel Obstetrics Wing. I'll have my people on it by the end of the evening."

The guards don't stop me. They let me go past, following the signs deeper into the hospital. *Fuck this,* my pounding heart says. *Fuck not being her family.* That was so difficult because I'm not Eva's husband. I'm not *family*.

But I don't care.

I don't care if she has thoughts about the proposal. I don't care if she's pissed at me. I don't care if she stays that way for the rest of her life.

Here's what I know. I wasn't there for her when she discovered she was pregnant. I still feel like a fucking asshole that she was alone for that.

I'm not going to let it happen again. Not this time. All through our fake relationship, I kept making the argument that Eva should do less for her family. I should have been doing more for her.

So to hell with staying away.

The signs lead me down several hallways, each quieter than the last, until I reach a nurses' station.

"I'm here for Haley Morelli."

I'm here for Eva, who is here for Haley. It's true, in a way.

The nurse points. "Other end of the wing."

Of course. Most hospitals have areas designated for VIP patients. People who require more privacy. More security. There's an entirely separate waiting room, a guard posted outside the door.

The sight of Eva in that waiting room stops me in my tracks.

She's dressed in soft, black clothes. Her hair is swept back in a neat twist. She looks fragile but strong with her hands on her sister Daphne's face. Daphne's husband stands at her side, his brow furrowed. It looks like they've just arrived.

Eva murmurs something to Daphne, then gives her a quick hug. Then Daphne and Emerson choose a seat. Daphne reaches out and squeezes her other sister's hand—Sophia. At the side of the room, the brother with the scar, Tiernan, waits with his arm around a woman. He lifts his chin and responds to someone across the way.

"I don't know. Ten minutes?"

Lucian, the oldest Morelli son, paces into view, his wife Elaine at his side. "It feels longer than that."

They disappear again as Tiernan says *sure as fuck does.*

Bryant and Sarah enter the room, the youngest Morelli with them. Sarah pats her hair, looking frazzled. Bryant reaches for Eva almost absently, then pulls her into his arms while she speaks to them in a low voice.

It stops my heart. A genuine hug from Bryant Morelli is shocking enough. But…they're all here. All of the Morellis, I think. Except for the brother who lives overseas, Carter.

They look…normal.

Like a regular family, despite all the money and power.

And Eva in the middle of it, keeping everyone

calm.

They need her.

I need her.

Needing her is all I'm thinking about as my feet carry me in. I need to be here for her. In whatever way I can.

I'm expecting a fuss when I cross the threshold. The guards converging on me. Eva, raising her chin and banishing me from the room with an imperious expression.

Except she's turned her attention to another person in the room. Phillip Constantine is here with his son, Cash.

"I'm not sure she'll be able to find us," Phillip says. "Petra might not know this wing."

Petra. Haley's older sister.

"If she has any trouble, we'll send someone to get her. Okay? We're only a text away."

Phillip sees me first. His eyebrows go up, as if he's trying to place me. We've met many times at Constantine events. "Oh," he says, after a beat. "Finn's here."

Eva turns her head.

My breath feels tight in my lungs. Tension pulls through the air. I want to go to her, but I know I have to let her come to me.

She pats Phillip's hand one more time, and

Cash tugs at his elbow. "Let's sit down, Dad."

Then Eva's walking toward me. I'd deserve to get kicked out. I would deserve any harsh words she wanted to say.

Our eyes lock.

I can't predict what she'll do, so I let it go. She's close. Closer still. I wait for her to speak to the guards. I wait for her to snap at me.

Instead, she tucks herself into my chest, her arms sliding around my waist.

Nothing has ever felt so right as closing my arms around her.

I can't breathe. My heart aches. My lungs hurt. *I missed you so much.* The words don't make it past the lump in my throat. It's not about me, anyway. It's not about how much I want her and how sorry I am that I fucked up.

I hold her without saying a word, rubbing her back as she trembles. Eva's not going to cry. Not when other people need her to be steady. But I can feel how worried she is. I can feel, from her head to her toes, how much she loves her family.

How much she could love me.

We don't need to speak. I can tell from the expression on her face—on all of their faces—that the birth didn't go as planned. That they're all anxious for their brother. Their son. His wife.

The baby.

This is what I should have done all along. I should have stood by her side. Held her in my arms.

Eva breathes deep. The tension in the room is palpable. Sarah hovers near a set of chairs, staring at the door into the patient wing. Bryant shoves his hands in his pockets and stands back near the wall. Lucian confers with him in a low voice, then goes back to his wife.

Daphne traces a pattern on the back of Emerson's hand. Sophia and Lizzy sit close together, whispering. Cash and Phillip Constantine keep starting a conversation, but it trails off.

It takes another minute for Eva to straighten up. When she does, Sarah notices. She comes over to us, her face set. "Hello, Finn. Thank you for being here."

"Mrs. Morelli." I put a hand on her shoulder. "Does anyone need anything? Food? Coffee?"

The corners of her mouth turn down. "News. But I don't think you can get that for us."

Phillip Constantine approaches next and sticks out his hand to shake. "Good to see you, Finn. It's been..." He drops his hand, glancing toward the door. "Haven't seen you in a while."

"How are things with your inventions?" Phillip was always the Constantine brother with the least interest in conventional business. From what I understand, it caused some tension over the years.

"Oh." He runs a hand through his hair. "They're fine. Just fine."

"I'm sure we'll hear something soon," Eva says.

He opens his mouth, then closes it again, settling for a nod. Then he returns to Cash.

"I'm so sorry." Everyone picks up their heads at the woman's voice. Haley's sister, Petra, rushes into the room, her eyes wide. "The nanny was gone for the day, and my husband—" She bites her lip at the mention of her husband. "I got here as soon as I could. How is Haley?"

"We'll find out any minute. Can I get you something to drink?" Eva puts her arm through Petra's and guides her over to where Cash and Phillip are waiting.

Everyone settles again. Eva steps into the next room—a kitchen. She returns a minute later with a can of Coke, which she gives to Phillip. He holds it in his hand but doesn't open it.

"I'm worried about her," he says to the can.

"We're all worried, Dad." Cash puts a hand on his arm. "But she's going to be okay. She's in good hands. That's what all the nurses keep saying, right?"

"Right," Eva agrees.

I've only been here a few minutes, but I'm already feeling the effects of this wait. The air in the waiting room seems thin. It wouldn't be right to lose ourselves in conversation. There's nothing to do but watch the seconds tick by.

My heartbeat *thud*s.

The only person who doesn't seem impatient, not at all, is Daphne's husband, Emerson. Daphne taps a foot on the floor. She holds his hand, the pad of her thumb tracing circles on his skin. How is he so calm? I'm pretending to be calm. I want this situation to have a happy ending. For Haley and Leo, of course, but also for Eva.

And if it's not a happy ending, I want to help her through whatever comes next.

I just need to know.

All my life, I've been filled with certainty. I knew, without a shadow of a doubt, that my mind would betray me long before my body gave out. I knew I'd become a burden on my caretakers. I knew I'd be hidden from the world while Hemingway did his best with Hughes Industries.

I thought that covered everything. Nothing

else could matter in the face of that bleak ending.

But it does.

Jesus, it does.

I'm about to flag down the nearest nurse and demand an update, never mind that I'm not family, when voices lift on the other side of the door. They get louder, approaching fast. Sarah grips Bryant's arm. Daphne gets out of her seat. Eva steps close to me, her breathing shallow.

The door to the patient wing swings open to reveal a doctor with a white coat over her blue scrubs. "—a few checks, but those can wait until after the first hour. You can do skin-to-skin in the recovery suite until the surgical team is finished with Haley."

She holds the door open, and Leo steps through. He's dressed in scrubs and there are tears in his eyes.

He has a tiny, *tiny* baby in his arms.

Nobody moves.

Leo clears his throat. "Haley's going to be okay. They're stitching her up right now. It went really well. Also, the baby is born."

Relief explodes over the room. Daphne shrieks. More than a few of them clap. Bryant makes the sign of the cross. Eva squeezes me tight around the waist. Everyone converges on Leo and the new baby, holding themselves back just far enough to give them both a little breathing room.

Eva pulls me closer to the clutch of her family, rising on tiptoe to see the baby's face.

I'm...choked up.

It's such a warm, human sensation that I feel a little drunk. I'm so relieved for this baby and her mother and for Leo and Eva and *all of them* that, for the first time, I get it.

I get why you'd have a child despite the fear. I still wouldn't choose it. Not for myself. But it's happening. Eva's pregnant, the baby is *ours,* and I'm okay with it.

She's beaming, and her happiness for her brother chokes me up *again.*

"Congratulations," I say to Leo over the press. Sarah leans in, gently touching the baby's cheek, the fold of her tiny, pink hat. "I don't know how you're holding it together. I'm going to be a wreck when our baby is born."

Leo winces.

The next second, my own words reach me.

Sarah freezes over her new granddaughter, her eyes wide.

Daphne speaks first. "Eva, you're *pregnant?*"

Then all hell breaks loose.

CHAPTER ELEVEN

Eva

HALEY RECLINES ON a mountain of pillows in her hospital bed, smiling down at her new baby daughter. Her hair came out black, like a true Morelli. She's a miniature of her father, lying perfect in her mother's arms. Leo watches from the side of the bed, reverent. In awe of his newborn. In awe of his wife.

Finally, a moment of peace.

There were questions after Finn's comment. A cascade of them that was abruptly cut off by Lucian, terse, saying *this baby was just born.*

The attention focused back on Leo and his newborn. He met my eyes over their heads and gave me a look that said *is this guy serious?*

Shortly after, he was whisked back to the recovery room. I found him there twenty minutes later. The rest of the family had been ushered out with promises of pictures and updates.

Leo was sitting in the room's rocking chair, his dress shirt on but unbuttoned. He'd taken off his T-shirt. The new baby dozed on his chest under a blanket printed with dinosaurs. I expected him to make a comment about how Finn had royally fucked up *that* announcement, but instead he said, *It'll be okay. I promise.*

We sat there for another hour, him doing skin-to-skin with the baby, until they brought Haley back. She was desperate to see both of them. Leo waited a tactful thirty minutes to break the news.

Haley's been quiet since. Understandable, since she had to figure out how to nurse. A lactation consultant bustled in and helped her position the baby. I think it's going okay.

The deep concentration slowly fades from Haley's face. She looks up from the baby and into Leo's eyes. "Would you give us a few minutes?"

He brushes a lock of hair away from her cheek. "No."

"Leo. I need some girl time. Go find something to eat. Stretch your legs."

My brother smiles at her quiet insistence, then leans down to kiss the top of the baby's head. He kisses Haley's cheek. Then he drags out his departure by fluffing her pillows and making sure Haley has the call button for the nurse, her phone, and an extra blanket.

"I love you," he says from the side of the bed.

"I love *you*." Haley smiles at him until he leans down and kisses her again. Her eyes follow him as he leaves. Then, with a little sigh, she looks at me. "I cannot *believe* you didn't tell me. Seriously. I'm kind of pissed."

My cheeks heat. "I know. I'm sorry. I just...I didn't believe it myself for a while there."

Haley looks back down at the baby. She's a tiny, perfect thing. "I have no idea if I'm doing this right," she murmurs.

"She looks happy. I'm not an expert, but I think you're doing great."

She focuses back on me, her expression cautious. "Are you upset because you aren't married?"

"Yes. No." I push my hair out of my face and lean back in the hospital chair. "I mean...I was raised with traditional values. We all were. I always just assumed that if I got pregnant, I would be married. I assumed I'd be creating a family, instead of..."

Instead of negotiating a business proposal. Instead of dwelling on the end, instead of the hope of a new life.

Haley's eyes glisten with a sheen of tears. "Does Finn…not want the baby?"

"Finn…" This moment seems extremely high-stakes. Finn's not here, but every word matters. "I don't want to bad-mouth him. I'm just not sure exactly how to explain the way he reacted."

My brother's wife presses a knuckle to the corner of her eyes. "You could try."

Careful, careful. "He didn't plan on having a child, so I think he was…he was pretty shocked. And his family history gives him some good reasons to be concerned. He's acting reasonably from his point of view. He's trying to offer me everything he can. His name. His money. Security."

Haley's eyebrows pull together. "But?"

"But he wants to maintain an emotional distance. An emotional wall. He was up front about it from the very first night. And…he ended things before I realized I was pregnant. He told me it was over and basically kicked me out of his house. I was the one who hoped for more."

"You weren't the only one."

I raise my eyebrows at her. "Yes, I was."

Those blue eyes flick toward the ceiling, but she's not mocking. "I've *seen* the two of you, Eva.

You can swear up and down that it was all a lie and you were the fool who fell in love, but Finn did, too."

"And how would you know that?"

"Because I've seen a man in love before."

"What, your sister's husband?"

This time, Haley gives me a *look,* a shadow flickering over her eyes. "My sister has what is essentially an arranged marriage. I'm not sure they've ever been in love. I'm talking about Leo, obviously."

"Obviously," I echo. But a man in love wouldn't have freaked out the way Finn did. A man in love wouldn't have been so cold. "But Leo never—"

"Told me it was over and kicked me out of his house? Yes, he did."

"He did *not.*"

"Daphne didn't tell you? She was there."

Oh, I am going to have a *stern* discussion with both Leo *and* Daphne. "She was vague about the details. I just knew that you had gone home, and Leo was…"

"Beside himself. Because he was in love with me. And maybe Finn's not in love with you, but I don't buy it. I think he is. But mostly, I'm happy for you. I wish you'd have told me. I want to be there for you, Eva. You've been here for me. It's a two-way street."

The baby stirs, one fist popping up in an uncoordinated stretch. She opens her eyes. I hold my breath, waiting for her raspy cry. But then her eyes close again, and slowly, slowly, she drifts to sleep.

We both admire her in silence for a little while.

"How was it? The birth, I mean."

Haley lets out a long breath and meets my eyes. "It was scary," she admits. "I didn't expect for labor to come on so fast. All the books said it would be gradual, but it wasn't. And it *hurt*." Her eyes get huge. "I mean, *wow*. Then we got here…"

She looks down at her daughter, and my heart squeezes.

"We got here, and things seemed okay. One minute, it was fine. The next, there were, like, six people in the room. I had to sign a paper in the middle of a contraction. And I just—I wanted to cry." Haley laughs. "I held it together, though. I thought Leo was going to chase us down the hall to the operating room if I shed even a single tear."

"Yeah. I think he would have."

"It was…not good, being in there alone. I

hated it. And the pain was so much worse once I wasn't with him. But everyone was kind. Once I was numb, it wasn't so bad. Then they let Leo come in, and then it was okay. It was good."

A tear slips down her cheek. Haley's chin quivers.

"It's okay. Whatever it is, you can tell me."

"I had hoped—" Haley breaks off, her voice thick. "I had hoped to just—to deliver her the way I imagined. I don't know. Maybe it would have been worse. But I didn't even get to try."

I take her hand and squeeze it. "I'm proud of you."

"Me too. I think I'm just still coming to terms with it. I'm *so* glad she's okay." More tears spill over, and Haley laughs. "I was more worried about her than anything."

"I'm so happy you're both here. I can't—" I have to fan at my own eyes. "I'm so glad every-thing's okay, Haley."

We both end up staring at the baby again.

I can't believe how much I love my new niece. Of course I expected to love her, but this feeling? *This?* I would kill for her. Die for her. And she's two hours old.

Haley's puffy from surgery. Her hair is in a slightly disheveled bun. She's clearly exhausted, but when she strokes her baby's cheek, her face shines with love. I feel indescribably lucky to be able to sit in the glow of it.

Which is why it might be worth it.

Even if Finn never sees my point of view, and even if he never comes around, our baby could be absolutely worth it. He can try to stay emotionally separate, if that's truly what he wants.

In that case, I wouldn't have *everything* that Haley does. But I'd still have the love of my child. And I'd love him to the moon and back.

"I guess it's probably time," Haley says.

"For me to go?"

She meets my eyes with a bright, teary smile. "No. Not unless you want to. I think it's time to tell you the news."

"Is there…more news? Other than that she's born?" My family is still reeling from Finn's big pregnancy announcement. If any other bombshells land tonight, I'll be forced to lie down.

I feel Leo enter the room behind me.

"It's okay," Haley says. "We'll talk more later."

"Did you tell her?" Leo comes to the side of the bed and slides on next to Haley, wrapping his arm carefully around her. He touches the baby's nose with the pad of his finger.

"Tell me what?" My mind spins a hundred possible scenarios. Something they've discovered about the baby now that she's born. Something to do with the family. His house? I'm hazy with the emotion of the day. I was *terrified.* I can admit it now that the uncertainty has passed.

"We chose her name." Leo traces a path down the baby's blanket to her tiny hand. It opens at his touch, and then her fist is wrapped tightly around his finger.

"You did?"

This scene is going to break my heart into a million pieces. It's too sweet, and I want it for myself too much. At the same time, I'm overwhelmed by joy for them. Real joy.

"Her first name is Abigail." Haley's voice is soft. Shy.

"*Abigail.*" I reach out and adjust her tiny pink cap. "I love it. Will you call her Abby?"

"Leo's been doing that for weeks. He practices calling for her when nobody's at the house."

Leo doesn't bother to look sheepish. "I did. But now she's here. It's the real thing."

"It's absolutely beautiful. Just like her." I can't keep the smile off my face. "Does she have a middle name?"

"Eva," Leo says.

I look up at him, my fingertip on Abby's cheek. His eyes have a rare sheen. "Yes?"

"Her middle name is Eva," Haley says. "After you."

CHAPTER TWELVE

Finn

I HAVE TO tell Hemingway that Eva's pregnant.

It's the number-one item on my agenda, aside from figuring out the rest of my life.

After the hospital, I go home and toss and turn in my bed. Dreading a conversation makes for excellent sleep and an even better day at the office. By five o'clock I'm overcompensating for how tired and surly I feel, forcing exaggerated politeness onto my staff until my secretary grits her teeth.

When I get home, I brace myself. If my father's having a bad day, I'm not sure I have the emotional fortitude to handle him and Hemingway at the same time.

But...

It's quiet.

No excuses left now.

I've spent years making sure Hemingway knew about safe sex. I had to make him understand that children were a terrible risk. Which is why it makes perfect sense that I'm the one who fucked up.

I can't let him hear through the grapevine like the engagement.

That was fake, anyway. This is real.

Fifteen minutes to change out of my work clothes and wash the day off in the shower. Then I go find him.

He's in the den, fingers flying over the keyboard of his laptop.

"Hem."

He glances up at me. "Hey." More typing. He pulls the laptop off the coffee table and into his lap. "I heard you rush out of here last night. What was that about?"

"I went to be with Eva." It's a relief to sit down on the couch across from him. Less of a relief to be hovering at the margins of this conversation. "Her niece was born."

"Is she okay?" Hem peers at me over the screen.

"She was a bit early, from what I can tell. It was tense for a while."

"But she's good now?"

"Yeah. Ten fingers, ten toes."

Hemingway makes a short sound of agreement and types some more.

God, I hate this. I hate it almost as much as being apart from Eva. Dragging my feet won't make it any easier. There's a lot of hard shit for someone who used to live for pleasure. Was it a hollow sort of pleasure? Sure, but it was better than pain. "There's something I need to tell you."

My brother groans, his hands going still. "Please, for the love of Christ, let it not be more safe sex talk."

"Oh, it is."

He flips the laptop shut. "Are you serious? I know about condoms, Finn. We've been over this. And over this. I'm going to wrap myself in twenty-seven rubbers and an umbrella before I have sex."

"It's not about condoms, specifically. It is about babies, though."

"What the fuck are you talking about?"

I glare at him. "Language."

He raises an eyebrow.

"Fine." I hold up both hands. "Listen. Eva's pregnant."

Hemingway cocks his head to the side.

"What?"

"She's pregnant."

"Eva Morelli?"

"Yes."

"Did she... cheat on you?"

My heart squeezes again. "She's pregnant with my baby."

Hemingway lets out a breath. He looks down at the floor for several beats, then back up at me. "Holy shit. I don't even know what to say. Are you...angry about it?"

"I'm not angry, but I'm not fine either." It's not my best moment, gritting my teeth to stop my emotions from pouring out all over my little brother. It's useless. They're already here. I never wanted this. I was trying to spare a future child my fate, and it's happening anyway. "If I had to nail down a single overriding emotion, I guess I'd say I'm fucking terrified."

"Language."

"I didn't use a condom."

There's no judgment in his brown eyes. They remind me of our father's. "Why?"

"Because I lose my head when I'm around her."

"Do you love her?"

I love her, which is why I have to get her away

from me. It's what I've done my whole life—kept my distance so that I don't hurt anyone when I become a husk of a human. "Yes."

Hemingway clasps his hands in front of him. "I'm scared, too."

My voice is hoarse. "Of what?"

"Of becoming like Dad. Obviously. That shit is scary. It's not good no matter how you look at it."

I'm completely out of my depth here. Never once in my life did I think I'd have to parent Hemingway about the impending birth of my child. But all the fatalistic shit I'm used to saying sticks in my throat. "According to Dad, we have some hope as long as we're still alive."

"I'm also afraid of becoming like you."

"Ouch."

"You seem so happy on the outside. Everyone believes it, but I know better."

"I know how hypocritical this is. I'm the one who's been drilling it into your head to use a condom, to hold yourself back. I'm the one who fucked this up."

Hemingway leans heavily against the back of the couch and stares out the window. He's within his rights to be pissed at me. For years, if he wants. Forever.

But when he speaks, his tone is thoughtful. "It's not that I didn't see your point. About not getting married and not having kids. About not carrying on the Hughes curse."

He meets my eyes without flinching.

In a blink, he's grown up. That's how it feels. Hemingway has seemed like a kid to me all his life, but he's growing up. Time passes without my permission. "But?"

He shrugs. "But it was more because I looked up to you, not because it was what I wanted. Secretly, I've always wanted it. The house with the picket fence. The two point five kids."

"Hemingway."

"The thing is, Finn, I'm not selfless like you." He cracks a smile that cuts to the quick. "I'm selfish. I want a family, even if it ends badly."

This is what Dad was talking about. *This.*

Hope blazes in Hemingway's eyes. He might have moved home only recently, but he's seen the things that influenced my decision. My younger brother is refusing to give up.

"I want you to have those things, too."

Maybe it's me. Maybe I'm the one who's been selfish. I've been fucking miserly with happiness and hope, always holding it up in front of Hemingway and saying, *you can never have this.*

Ever. It was decided before you were born.

Maybe that's what I've been telling myself.

He's skeptical. "Eva got pregnant, so you changed your mind about everything?"

"Not about everything, but I want you to be happy. I've always wanted that."

"Yeah, but I always knew how you defined happiness. The parties and the yachts and fucking random people. I want what you have with Eva. A family."

The family I got in spite of what a bastard I've been. She thinks I don't want the baby. She thinks I don't want *her*, but the truth is, I want them too much. Who am I to sit here and tell Hemingway whether to have children? What gave me the right? "I'm sorry I ever tried to convince you otherwise."

Hemingway peers at me. "So are you happy? Or are you freaking out?"

"I'm…" I can't say *happy*. "I know what's coming for me."

He's silent, watching me. "Do you, though?"

A laugh escapes. "That's the curse, Hem. There's no way it can ever be broken. It's coming for me. And no matter how much I hate it, it's coming for you. The only thing we get to decide is what we do in the few years we have left."

"You could be wrong, you know."

I sigh. "Hem."

"I'm serious. I know how smart you are. How you brought Hughes Industries to new heights. How you manage a million different things to keep the secret in the age of social media. I know you're smart, but Finn, you're so freaking stupid sometimes."

"No, no. Don't hold back. Tell me what you really think."

"Because no matter how smart you are, you can't tell the future. No one can."

We'll have to agree to disagree on that one. I know the future, because I can read the past. It's like watching a row of dominoes fall, one by one. You know what's going to happen to the last domino.

Not because you have a crystal ball.

You know because it's physics. It's science. It's cause and effect.

I don't want to argue with Hemingway, though. And I don't want to be the reason he doesn't have a family, if that's what he wants. So I swallow my arguments of logic and science. I search for something I could say, some way to show him that we're not enemies, even if we don't agree.

"I'm trying to make a better future," I say, finally.

Not exactly an enthusiastic promise, but it's the truth.

Even without believing it's possible, I've kept fighting for Hemingway's health. And now I'll keep fighting for the baby's health. I'll keep donating money and supporting research. I'll keep pushing science along like Sisyphus with his goddamn boulder up a hill, knowing it'll roll back down.

Hemingway stands, and I'm not sure what he's doing until the moment he offers me his hand and pulls me up from the couch. Then he throws his arms around me. "Congratulations, asshole," he says into my ear. "I hope you don't fuck it up, because this is more than you deserve."

I already *have* fucked it up. But I don't say that to Hemingway.

"What's more than you deserve?" Our mother's voice startles us both.

We both turn to watch her breeze in, fixing her hair as she comes.

Geneva Hughes has white-blonde hair and blue eyes and innate charisma. She looks like she could be an old Hollywood actress with high cheekbones and a tulle gown. She sweeps across the den and kisses my cheek, then Hemingway's, smelling faintly of ocean spray.

The last time I saw her, I visited her home in Prague to break the news that I was letting Hem come home from boarding school. She didn't like it. She thought he should live apart from my father, the same way she lives apart from him.

She can't stand the heartbreak of seeing him broken, and she thinks we can't stand it either.

But I *can* stand the pain. The realization hits me like an eighteen wheeler.

I stand the pain so my father doesn't have to face this alone. Which makes me wonder why I've been pushing Eva away. Maybe life is just a journey through heartache. It's coming for me anyway. I can't escape it. That's the irony. Pushing Eva away hasn't made me avoid it. It's still here.

Maybe the pain is worth it.

Hemingway pushes a hand through his hair. "Hey, Mom."

"Is someone going to tell me what's going on?" My mother sweeps her hands around the room. It's like she just stepped out to look at her flowers in the garden. She has the air of a person who's been gone for a few hours, not a few years. It feels, somehow, like she belongs here rather than her hundred vacation homes around the world.

My brother points at me. "He knocked up Eva Morelli."

"Phineas. Is he joking?"

I'm going to punch him. "No. He's not."

A slow nod. "This explains the engagement. The number of texts I get, my God. Everyone angling for information. Everyone trying to get an invitation to the wedding. I just smile and pretend to be mysterious, when the truth is I don't even know if *I'll* be invited to the wedding."

I feel the smallest twinge of guilt. My mother wasn't included in planning for the engagement because no one was. It was supposed to end before it became anything real.

Now there's a baby on the way. My baby.

"I'm sorry."

"No phone call. No text. Not even an email. I don't know where I was supposed to find out. How are kids sharing information these days? Do you have a TikTok account?"

I deserve that. "I should have told you. Is that why you came?"

"*What is your new daughter-in-law like?* they ask. Oh, yes, of course we've met, I say. But it's been almost a decade. I remember a serious young woman with dark eyes. Obedient. So busy managing her parents that I doubted she had any room for being a child. You have that in common, I suppose."

My heart squeezes. She was serious, wasn't she? I was so busy having fun that I barely noticed. Like Hemingway said, I defined happiness as parties and yachts and fucking random people. "Of course you've met Eva."

"What does she look like now? *Beautiful*, I say. Because I can find some photos from the society websites as well as anyone. What does she do? *Oh, she's so accomplished. Very philanthropic. She manages the Morelli Fund.*" My mother's voice has become shrill. "It's on their Wikipedia page."

"I should have told you."

"Tell me now, Phineas. Why Eva? Why a Morelli?"

Christ. The Morelli family has been in a longstanding feud with the Constantines. For decades. And Caroline Constantine is my aunt. My mother's sister. "They've repaired the rift between the families."

She waves this away. "I've heard those rumors. I know about the little Morelli-Constantine children being born. I don't know why Caroline has allowed it. It's not going to end well."

"The Hughes are Switzerland in that feud, anyway," I say, this time with a hint of warning.

As head of the family I have this power—even over my mother. She would prefer that the Hughes family get involved, that we officially side with the Constantines. That would only make us smaller. The Hughes family is above the feud. My father saw the wisdom of that.

She gives me a dark look. "Still, a Morelli? My God. They're so...Catholic."

That makes me smile. I wonder if Eva wants me to convert. Probably. I imagine myself in swim trunks and a baby pool getting baptized. Then my smile fades. That's assuming I can repair things between us. That's assuming I even want to. Looking at my mother reminds me of why I might not want to. It's one thing to accept my own pain. It's another to inflict it on someone else.

"Though I suppose with a baby on the way, there's no choice," my mother continues. "At least she'll be an obedient daughter-in-law."

I can't help it. I snort. "*Obedient* is not a word I'd use to describe Eva."

My mother's expression turns grave. "Does she know?"

"She does."

"I suppose she thinks marrying a Hughes is worth it."

"She doesn't need money. Or power. She's already rich and powerful."

"It would be better if she did need those things. It would be better if she only cared about the Hughes name, because that's all she'll have once the curse takes you."

My throat feels tight. "Right."

"I'd like to meet her. She should know what she's getting into."

I can just imagine that. "The timing isn't good right now."

"She should know how it feels to watch the man you love waste away to nothing."

"Geneva!" My father comes in through the door, wearing his pajamas, his hair askew. He looks like a tired, faded version of himself, except for the eyes. In his eyes there's only delight. He recognizes her. Fuck, he *recognizes* her. There was only a fifty-percent chance of that happening. And why is he even wandering around the house? "I've been looking everywhere for you."

To her credit, she doesn't miss a beat. She kisses Dad's cheek and gives him a quick, gentle hug. She could have come home from one of her old spa days. "Hello, Daniel. I'm right here."

"And looking absolutely radiant. Where have you been?"

"Oh, out and about." She manages a breezy smile, but I can sense the strain. I see the pain underneath. The same way Hemingway saw the pain beneath my playboy façade. The Hughes aren't that great at hiding it. "A little bit of shopping. I visited a friend. Am I in time for dinner?"

I clear my throat. I never expected to see both of my parents in the same room again. It's bittersweet, this moment. Because it can't last. "It should be ready now, actually."

"Let's not keep it waiting." Dad escorts Mom out of the den. "I'm starving."

She smiles at him, though I can see the sorrow in her eyes. "How was your day?"

"Busy. Very busy. It's going to be one of our best quarters ever." He grins at her, a ghost of the competent mogul he once was. "There's this new trend that's going to change the world. Something called social media. Some people think it's a fad, but I already know it's going to be huge."

Hemingway and I trail behind them as they go to the kitchen. From this vantage point, I can see my mom turn her head. This is ostensibly to look into the other rooms we're passing. I catch the corners of her mouth turning down and the quiver in her chin. It's hidden when she faces my father again.

"It sounds wonderful."

He keeps up his chatter while we take our seats at the table.

We have a small staff for the size of the house.

Only one chef, one housekeeper, and one groundskeeper.

The less people here, the less people who need to know our secrets. One of my father's evening nurses is here. Jennifer hovers at a respectful distance, allowing us privacy while also being nearby in case my father needs assistance. Half of the time, he refuses to eat. *I'm not hungry*, he says. This time, he beams down at braised chicken and green beans with a side of glazed carrots and proclaims it *wonderful.*

I can feel the seconds ticking away, closer and closer to evening. To sunset.

Dad makes it through dinner. Through dessert. I manage to hold his attention with a story about one of my racehorses, texted to me from one of the trainers at our property upstate.

He laughs about Pegasus Gold's thirst for victory on the racetrack. That's when I see the first shadow of confusion in his eyes.

Hemingway sees it, too. He stiffens in his seat.

"Where…" Dad's forehead wrinkles. "Where is the coffee? We always have coffee with dessert."

"I gave it up," my mother answers. "I get heartburn if I have it after three in the afternoon."

"We're okay without coffee, Dad. It'll keep me up all night. And I think we're all done eating, so—"

"We always have coffee. I had the cook brew a pot. What's taking so long? Geneva doesn't like to wait around at the table."

"I'm fine, Daniel. Really." My mom pats his hand.

He frowns at her touch, following her fingertips up her arm to her face.

He's glaring by the time he meets her eyes. "Who the hell are you?"

"Daniel." She keeps her voice very, very calm. "It's me. Your wife."

"Don't lie to me." Spots of color appear high on his cheeks. "I'm not married, and I'd know, wouldn't I? I've never seen you before. What are you doing in my house?"

"Dad." His eyes dart toward mine. "Mom came over to have dinner with us."

"Why didn't you tell me? Where is she?"

"Daniel—"

He shoots out of his chair, knocking it over in the process. "You are not my wife. *She* is not my wife. Who let you in here?"

"Dad, it's okay." Hemingway stands up and moves around the other side of the table. He's in Dad's range before I can warn him back. "*Dad.*"

My father rounds on Hemingway, his body rotating into the slap. It turns clawed before it reaches the side of Hemingway's head and makes audible contact.

Hemingway jerks back, clapping his hand to his head. "I'm okay." His cheek is bright red. "Finn. I'm fine."

My pulse pounds like Dad hit me instead, over and over again. Adrenaline clarifies my horror and doubles it. I know what I'm watching. I'm watching myself, twenty years from now. I'm watching my son grab at the side of his head, blinking, bewildered. I'm watching Eva try to intervene.

I'm almost there, I'm *almost* there, but my mother is in the way. "Daniel. Don't touch him."

He lunges for her. Their limbs get tangled. I see his fist in her hair and terrified fury in his brown eyes.

I shove myself between my parents. Dad's efforts make it harder to unhook his hands from my mother's hair. She steps back, then back again.

He's yelling, eyes wide with distress. "Who let a stranger into this house?"

"Dad. *Dad*. It's okay. I know her." He's doing his best to reach around me. I don't know what the hell he's planning. My heart races. Jennifer appears at the dining room door. If he won't listen to me, she's next up. She pulls her phone from her pocket and sends a text. The second nurse on shift will have to help if neither of us is enough. "She's not a stranger."

"I don't know her, Phineas. She's an imposter. Take her away. Make her leave."

"Okay, Dad. Okay. Calm down. *Please.*"

He struggles, but the fight leaves him. Jennifer approaches and puts a gentle hand on his arm. "Mr. Hughes, I made some herbal tea. Would you like some? I could put on *Jeopardy* in the living room."

"Fine." He pushes away from me, getting distance. I stay where I am in case he makes a final attempt. "That's fine. I don't want to miss the categories."

"Good timing, then. You haven't." Jennifer takes his arm. "It starts in two minutes."

It starts whenever she plays the recorded episodes.

I keep my eyes on them while they leave.

Then I go to my brother and put an arm around his shoulders. Turn his head to see if Dad left any marks. There are thin, red scratches at his temple, but nothing deep.

"I'm sorry, Hem. I should have intervened earlier."

"It's really fine. He didn't hurt me."

Mom approaches, taking her turn at inspecting Hemingway's wounds. He holds still for her until she releases him. Does she feel as guilty as I do?

The tremble in her voice says *yes*. "I'll take my usual suite, if that's all right, Finn."

"Of course, Mom."

The heavy quiet in the dining room steals my breath.

This kind of evening is why I decided never to have children. It's a stark reminder of what Eva faces if I allow her to stay with me. I don't know how I can let her do it.

And I don't think I can stop her.

CHAPTER THIRTEEN

Eva

EVEN FILLING OUT the forms at the doctor's office feels surprisingly emotional.

Age? *33.*

Is this your first pregnancy? *Yes.*

Any family history of miscarriages, low birth weight, etc? *My mother had three miscarriages.*

Apparently, miscarriages are common. So common that many women don't know they've had one. It seems like a small miracle that I'm pregnant at all, given that.

I work my way through the pages, feeling faintly ill. Morning sickness, probably. There's a packet of Club crackers in my purse now. I slip one out and eat it, but the sensation doesn't go away.

I'm nervous. That's what this is.

I'm sure of the baby. I *want* the baby. But the form seems like a catalog of all the ways that this might not be ideal. I know the doctors just want as much information as possible. I also know that a perfectly normal pregnancy can still end in an urgent C-section, like it did for Haley.

I take the clipboard with the completed forms back to the reception desk. I'm just sinking into my seat when the outer door opens, letting in a breath of warm air.

It's not another woman here for an appointment.

It's Finn.

He's dressed in a dark suit that's custom tailored to his muscles. My body flushes at the sight of him. A suit and tie is nothing special. It's what he would wear any day at the office.

Except he's not at the office.

He takes the seat next to me. The flush turns hot and indignant and...relieved.

Finn nods at me. "Morelli."

"Morelli? Oh my God. How did you know I was here?"

Finn pats my hand as if I have gone slightly 'round the bend. "I have spies all throughout this city."

It's impossible to express how badly I want to

hold his hand, but I do not. I fold mine in my lap, instead. I'm self contained. No man is an island, but this woman? She is. "That's stalkerish."

"Well, you didn't marry me, so this is how it has to be." He flashes me a smile. *I'm interested.* I can almost hear his voice the way it was in the poker club. Hot. Smooth. Neither of us was forcing anything. "I'm not walking away."

"Listen, I was going to tell you the results."

"Now you don't have to, because I'm here." I move to turn away, to collect myself, but Finn puts a hand on my arm. "We haven't had a chance to talk about what happened."

"Nothing happened."

"I told your entire family that you're pregnant, and the baby is mine."

"They'd have found out sooner or later." Would they have freaked out quite so much? Probably not. But what's done is done. The cat is, as they say, out of the bag. "Why are you here?"

A hint of his usual charming grin lifts the corner of his mouth, then disappears. "Do you think I only show up for your brother's baby? Not yours? Not ours?"

"That was different. That was an emergency. And I did appreciate having you there." My heart twists. "But this is—this is just confirmation about a baby you don't want."

"My feelings about the baby—" Another patient exits the office. Finn's eyes stay on mine as she goes past. "My feelings about the baby won't affect my support for you. Or for the child."

"Finn."

"You're right. I didn't plan on this. I didn't want this to happen. But I'm here for the baby."

"And for me?"

"I'm going to take care of you, Eva."

Duty. Responsibility. One thing I know about Finn Hughes is that he's a man of honor. He'll take care of what he feels he should, regardless of whether he wants to. "Because you have to."

"Because any half-decent man would take care of his child and the mother of his child. That includes attending your doctor appointments, if you'll let me."

He's so careful to put the baby between us. I'm no longer Eva Morelli, desirable woman. I'm the mother of his child. It's a position of honor, but not a position of intimacy.

On some level I know it's a good thing that he's willing to step up, even for a child he didn't initially want. He's a good man, though he probably wouldn't like me to point it out.

On the other hand, I can't help but yearn for

having him in a different capacity. Not only as the father of my child, but as my life partner. As my husband.

The door to the patient area opens. A red-haired woman in sleek pink scrubs steps out. "Eva Morelli?"

Finn stands at the same time I do, putting his hand on the small of my back, as casual as any husband protecting his pregnant wife. There's a challenge in his hazel eyes. And in the quirk of his lips. *Kick me out right now. Otherwise, I'm going with you.*

I'm too nervous to argue right now. I want him to be here too much to demand that he leave.

It's his baby, too. Our baby.

The air between us heats. Finn is perfectly composed, his hands in his pockets.

"Come on, let's go." I let a note of impatience show in my voice as if he's the one who made us stand there for an extra thirty seconds.

Finn follows me through the softly swinging door. He hangs back while I step onto a scale in a discreet alcove. The nurse in pink scrubs shows us to a comfortable room done up in warm neutrals. An ultrasound machine hums in one corner. I take the soft, sterile sheet she offers me and nod along with her instructions.

"The doctor will be back in a minute." She leaves with a bright smile.

I go to the low padded bench across the room from the exam table and unzip my slacks.

"Do you...want me to turn around?" Finn asks.

"Are you afraid to see me half-naked?" I've been through this routine every year since I was sixteen. The difference is that there wasn't a baby. It's the work of fifteen seconds to strip off my pants and panties and fold them on the bench. I whirl the sheet around my waist as a final step. "There. I'm decent."

I turn to face Finn and find him staring, his eyes hot with longing.

"This isn't sexy, Finn."

"No, of course not." He clears his throat and we change places. Finn sits next to my clothes on the bench. I take my place on the exam table.

My heart pounds.

Finn opens his mouth, but he's interrupted by a brisk knock on the door. The doctor enters with the pink-scrubbed nurse. There's a review of my medical history. Confirmation of the details I wrote on the form. And then the doctor is explaining the *kind* of ultrasound they'll do because it's so early in the pregnancy. Finn's eyes go from their faces to the wand at the side of the ultrasound machine.

"Is that—"

"Safe for the baby? Of course." The doctor continues without missing a beat. She pulls up a stool. The nurse dims the light and moves the ultrasound monitor so I can see it if I look up.

"Who did you bring with you today?" Her voice is softer now that she's got a hand under the sheet and a wand entering my body.

"This is Finn Hughes. He's the—the father."

A kind smile. "Dad, if you want to come to Eva's other side, you'll be able to see, too."

Finn gets up from his seat, his face set. He comes to the side of the table.

I won't abandon you, Finn. I can taste the words now. Letting him be part of this moment feels like keeping that promise, even if I'm not obligated to keep it anymore.

Even if the tension between us is so thick I can hardly breathe.

I reach for his hand in the glow of the ultrasound machine and thread my fingers through his.

He holds on tight.

We're both transfixed by the image on the screen. An oblong pool of black veers from side to side as the doctor moves the wand.

And there, near the edge—

"That's the fetus. Let me check to make sure there are no roommates."

Finn's hand clamps down on mine. Twins were never included in my thoughts about *the baby*.

The wand moves. The doctor searches.

"One for the money," she says with a low laugh, and I feel Finn's breath go out of him. His grip on my hand relents. No twins. "But not two for the show. Now I need to get some measurements."

The doctor taps at a keyboard below the monitor. The number of weeks and days of the baby's life appears on the screen. Lines cross the tiny bean in the black space.

The doctor turns a switch on the keyboard, and the room is filled with the rapid *whoosh-thud* of a heartbeat. "The heart tones sound normal. Healthy. Everything looks good here. We've got a few weeks to go until the heart is finished developing."

I can't stop staring. The baby is barely baby-shaped yet. I can just make out the curl of a head. A printer *whirrs*. The lights go back up. Finn helps me sit. The nurse steps out, and the doctor rolls her stool to the counter and adds notes to my file.

She smiles at me again, her gaze assessing. "You're about seven weeks along. We'll want you back at ten weeks to check your progress. In the meantime…" A pamphlet appears, tugged out of a holder on the countertop. "Here's a list of foods you'll want to minimize from your diet, especially in the first trimester. Have you already started taking prenatal vitamins?"

"No. I'll do that. Is there a brand you recommend?"

"Many of my patients have good luck with these." The doctor adds a note to the pamphlet, then hands it to me along with the ultrasound pictures. I'm struck by the image of the baby all over again.

She outlines the appointment schedule. The twenty-four hour hotline. Writes her personal cell phone number on the pamphlet next to her recommendation for prenatal vitamins.

"We'll be with you every step of the way. And you should know, Eva, that I research and recommend the most up-to-date best practices, but some of the more common pregnancy advice is a holdover from the nineteen-fifties. If you want clarification on anything, please ask."

"That sounds good. I don't really want pregnancy tips from the fifties."

She laughs. "What else would you like to talk about today?"

"When can we find out the sex of the baby?"

The doctor nods. "Some couples choose to wait until the twenty-week anatomy scan, but—"

"It's a boy." Finn's voice startles me. Both of his hands are shoved into his pockets. All his charm is hidden behind an angry scowl. *A boy with the Hughes curse.* He doesn't say it out loud.

He doesn't have to. I hear it loud and clear. "Finn."

"At your next appointment, we can do a blood draw and run a genetic test. We need time for the concentration of fetal DNA to reach viable levels. So that's…three or four weeks from now, plus a week for processing. That's how soon you can find out the gender."

"We already know it's a boy. What more is the test going to tell us?" Finn's sharp now.

"Genetic testing tells us whether the fetus might have certain disorders."

"Like what?"

She lists a bunch of things that sound terrifying. I don't want my baby to have any of those things. Maybe I understand Finn better now that

I feel this fear. Because this? This is only about the tiny possibility of disease. The potential. Finn believes the Hughes curse is a certainty.

"These things are unlikely," she says. "But some parents like to know."

"What does it mean if the test is positive?"

"It's not a certainty. These are only genetic markers. But if the risks are elevated, we can decide to do a diagnostic screening. That can be slightly more invasive."

He frowns. "What the fuck does that mean?"

"*Finn.*"

"I want to know what it means."

"This is why I didn't want to bring you."

The doctor folds her hands in her lap. "For diagnostic screening, we'd need cells from the fetus or the placenta or both. The procedure is relatively low risk, but we still wait for something to appear on genetic testing before we do it."

"And what would that change? If you found something, we wouldn't be able to fix it, would we?"

"No, there are very few treatments we can begin while the fetus is in utero. The tests are an option if the two of you would like more information about the baby. They're not mandatory. I want you to understand that. It's your choice as parents to have these screenings done."

"Great. Excellent. It's all pointless, then."

"Mr. Hughes." Somehow, this woman has managed to soften even more. "I know this can be scary to think about. I don't like to alarm parents, but I do like you to be informed."

"I want to know," I say, because it's true.

Finn gives me a dark look that says, *We already know the fate of this baby.*

"Most likely the tests will come back negative. But if they don't, they'll allow you to research the possibility of the condition before he or she is born."

"Or terminate the pregnancy." Finn's words echo in the small doctor's office. The fluorescent lights suddenly feel too bright. The hum of the ultrasound machine feels like a roar. "That's why people have those tests done, right? So they know whether to have an abortion?"

"Sometimes," the doctor says. "Sometimes they do wish to terminate. It's very unlikely that anything would show up. And again, we don't have to do it."

"Which way is better, doctor? Should we let someone suffer or pull the plug?"

I don't know whether to rage at Finn or hug

him. He's being a complete asshole.

He's spiraling, right in front of me.

The doctor doesn't look fazed. I'm guessing Finn isn't the first expectant father to have a meltdown at one of these appointments, but that doesn't make it better. "That's not an easy question. And it's not mine to answer. At least not for this pregnancy. It's about your personal beliefs. And your values."

"You know what I value?" he says. "Ignorance. It's bliss. That's what they say, isn't it? Information is overrated. Does anyone actually feel better seeing a positive result? That's bullshit. They don't. They always feel worse. The only reason to take the test is because you're hoping it's negative."

I'm stricken, because he's right. Sometimes information is overrated. Like the Hughes curse. It makes Finn sure of what will happen. Is it true? Maybe, maybe not. Either way, he's refusing to live a normal life. If he didn't know his destiny, if he was ignorant of the curse, he could love me. He could marry me. He could dream of a future. That's a hard truth to face.

"You're right," I tell him, my voice tight. "I don't want the test. I don't want to know."

"Will that make it better?" He barks a laugh.

"You know what? Maybe it's for the best that I don't attend any more of these appointments. I'll leave it to the experts. You have everything figured out."

"Finn." I reach for his hand, and he pulls himself out of reach.

"No, Eva. I'm not going to ruin this for you. You should have exactly the pregnancy you want. The happy little doctor appointments and the happy little ultrasounds."

A *fake* pregnancy. That's what he means. The baby is real, but the fantasy pregnancy where there's no future illness looming over us? That doesn't exist for Finn.

I'm covered by a sheet, but I'm not going to shrink from this. "I want you here, Finn. As the father of this child. As the man I love. But I don't want you here like this."

"Like what?"

"Angry."

"That's who I am underneath all the bullshit. That's who I am when I'm not wearing a tux and drinking champagne at a society event. Angry. I'm sorry if you didn't know that before I fucked you."

The doctor turns to me, her expression gentle. "Do you want me to ask him to leave? Because I can."

Tears sting my eyes. "No, please. I'm so sorry. He's just upset. Please give us a moment."

She gives him a severe look. "I'm going to be right outside. Holler if you need me."

Then she's gone, leaving a vacuum where the only calm in the room had been. Finn's gone off the deep end, and me? My heart is breaking. I take a deep breath.

Finn's caught in the endless loop of his fears, and I'm not sure I can show him the way out.

I'm not entirely sure there *is* a way out.

His hopelessness is seeping into me, moment by moment.

But—no. I refuse to feel hopeless about my child. About *our* child. I refuse.

A man broke me years ago. I won't let it happen again.

He's the one who speaks first. "You're getting a raw deal with me, Eva. I know it. You know it. Now the doctor knows it, too. I don't have a defense, but I did warn you."

That's who I am underneath all the bullshit. That's who I am when I'm not wearing a tux and drinking champagne at a society event. Angry. I'm sorry if you didn't know that before I fucked you.

I think I did know. Not at the beginning,

when he took me out to save me from my mother's machinations. Not then. But later, I started to see the real Finn underneath. I saw him, and it made me want him even more. I don't want the uncomplicated, shallow playboy. I want the grieving man inside, but I don't know how to reach him. The Hughes curse stands between us.

"Do you want an abortion?" I ask, my voice hoarse. I don't know if I can give it to him. I don't think I can, but I have to know if it's what he wants. Even if it feels like being flayed open with knives.

He curses and paces away from me—once, twice. That's as far as he can go in the small examination room.

"No." Finn doesn't look at me. He's facing the door, but I can hear him loud and clear. "If I believed it was better to pull the plug, if that's what my beliefs and my values really were, I would have killed myself a long time ago. If I thought it was better to avoid it, I'd already be gone."

My throat is too tight to speak. This means he's thought about it.

It means he considered it, with that casual Finn recklessness. Is that what the underground gambling and fights are really about? About risking a life he doesn't value?

About ending his life before he gets to the curse?

I can't imagine him gone. It hurts that he even once thought about ending his life. That he felt that kind of pain. I want to comfort him, even though he decided to stay.

Now I understand better how much this is costing him.

He decided to live, but only under those narrow parameters. Only as the playboy.

"I'll tell the doctor to come back in," he says, and walks out of the room.

CHAPTER FOURTEEN

Finn

M Y OFFICE AT Hughes Industries is the set for the greatest performance of a lifetime.

A custom Eames executive chair cushions my ass while I swivel between hard copy paperwork and my keyboard, pretending that my mind is completely absorbed in my work.

In other words, pretending to be normal.

This is my whole life. The expensive chair. A brand-new, top-of-the-line computer. Emails landing in my inbox every second. Contracts and mergers and personnel.

Really, it's marking days on the calendar and *pretending*.

It's been this way for years. When my dad started to decline, I increased my time in the office. I tried to keep it gradual so that people wouldn't ask too many questions. I kept his visits more regular. Then, as the years went by, I spaced them out. Pushed the boundary by a week here. Two weeks there.

I'll have to tell Hemingway how to do this. How to make it seem like I didn't just disappear.

I even start to type it out in an email, then delete it.

I'm not sending my brother a fucking memo on how to orchestrate my slow fade from the company. I'll talk to him about it in person. Later.

For now, it's another day on the job. A normal one. It's never been very normal, though. Most of the C-Suite executives are older guys. I'm the odd one out. I'm too young, not even thirty. I don't fit the profile of a CEO of a conglomerate this large.

And yet I am the boss, in all but the official title.

I'm a good boss, too. Hughes Industries regularly evaluates the company culture and employee satisfaction. The people who work for me describe me as kind, fair, and professional.

I'm none of those things today. I feel like a racehorse who's finally snapped and run away from his trainer. From his life.

I feel like screaming.

That would be a performance. Stalking through the office. Ripping up papers. Taking people by the shirt and demanding to know how they live with the future hanging over them like a boulder.

I didn't sleep well enough to sustain it. I'm not that person, anyway. I don't have a legendary temper. If I did, I'd keep it buried down deep. Hughes men can't afford to call attention to their personalities like that. It would only make it more noticeable when I started to change.

Instead, I type out email responses and send them. I review reports. I sign company documents.

All of this is shit I could do in my sleep. Things I *have* done while I'm half-awake from being up with my dad or being out all night.

The pretending is harder today. Eva's appointment is like a rock in my chest. I feel hobbled by the memory.

I lost it in there.

It was supposed to be a happy moment, and I couldn't stand it. Nobody is better at pretending than I am, but with Eva gazing at the little bean on the monitor and everyone cooing over a doomed child, I couldn't.

And she didn't understand. Eva Morelli is a fighter to the core. She's not going to give up just because the facts are against her.

It's not a kind thought to have. I wouldn't have it except my head is throbbing and Eva is pregnant and I am a disaster.

I know that tens of thousands of people depend on Hughes Industries. I know that the business we conduct has a meaningful impact on their lives.

In the end, it's a joke. Working for Hughes Industries can't save them. Being rich as hell can't save me. It won't be much longer until this all falls apart. Until it's Hemingway's turn in this office.

Knuckles rap at the doorframe. "Come on in."

"Am I interrupting?" Kevin is one of the C-Suite guys. Older than me, like all the other ones. A father.

"Not at all. What can I do for you?"

Kevin takes the seat across from me. "I wanted to ask if you're doing okay, Mr. Hughes. You've been quieter than usual today."

Finn, I want to say. *Just call me Finn, for Christ's sake.* I don't want to be Mr. Hughes yet. I don't want to be at the end of my life.

"Yes, of course. I'm doing well."

I can tell from his nod that Kevin doesn't believe me. "My door's always open if you want to run anything by me."

"Thank you." I wait long enough that it sounds genuine. "Did anything else come up?"

"I wanted to let you know I'll be out early on Friday."

This man doesn't have to run his personal time by me, and we both know it. "Something special happening?"

"My youngest is graduating from college. Sarah." Kevin pulls out his wallet and shows me a photo of a girl with curly hair and his eyes. "I'm so proud of her. It's the best day of my life when my kids graduate."

"Oh, yeah?"

"Those years of school feel so long, and then they're gone in the blink of an eye. All the homework and arguments and sports practices—" He laughs. "It all led up to this. Friday's going to be one of my most amazing days as a father."

My stomach sinks. "She'll be off to her new life, then?"

"God, yes. And she's so ready. Sarah was so cautious and quiet as a girl. Now she's come into her own. That's the reward. Seeing her so happy makes the hard times worth it."

I won't see the reward of raising a child.

If I'm lucky, I'll be aware enough to witness half of his childhood.

The appropriate thing to do is to congratulate Kevin again and make a note to send a card for his daughter. My chest is so tight with grief that it takes all my focus to keep sitting at my desk.

It's simple. Jesus. *Congratulations. See you on Monday.*

Stand up. Shake his hand.

"Would you do it all again?" I can't stop asking this question any more than I can stop feeling like shit about the appointment. "If you knew it would end badly?"

Kevin's brow furrows. "Do you mean with her career? Visual arts isn't what I would have chosen for her, but that part isn't up to me."

Visual arts. My child—my son, I'm sure the baby is my son—won't have the chance to become an actor or an artist. He'll have to be prepared to take Hemingway's place at Hughes Industries. I'll never have the chance to fret that he won't be successful at experimental art or music or film. He'll have no choice but to be good at *this*.

At pretending.

"I mean everything. Not just her career."

Kevin looks me in the eye. He's seriously considering his answer, I think. Then, finally:

"Yes."

Is it everyone else in the world? Would they all take the chance? Am I the only one who's selfish enough or self-aware enough to want to avoid the pain.

"Really?"

He spreads his palms flat on the desk.

"Well, look." Kevin uses a calm, sincere tone. It's the way I wish my father could speak to me all the time. "We don't get to know the ending. That's not how it works."

Okay. I *am* the only one. I've been saying it over and over, and nobody believes me.

Maybe I'm already losing my mind.

"I'm sure it'll turn out great for Sarah." I stand up and offer Kevin my hand. We shake. The pleasantries on his way out float over my head.

I could put in another hour of performing normalcy, but I don't sit down at my desk. Wandering down to the trading floor seems like a better idea. It's noisier, with more adrenaline. The guys down here are young and hungry. They can't see the finish line looming up ahead.

It's a floor packed with wealthy, smart professionals, which means that some of the society people I've partied with are here. They're still frat brothers, still dudes, well after college.

"Finn, my dude." A guy named Zach slaps me on the shoulder as a small crowd gathers. Familiar faces. Ones I don't care about at all. "Where have you been? Too busy dating Eva Morelli to come see us?"

He smirks, and I lose my grip on the jovial boss persona. "Don't say her fucking name."

Four other guys have closed in, and they all lean back. An uncertain tension cools the air. Zach exchanges a glance with one of his buddies Matt, who raises his eyebrows.

"It's good to see you." Matt's going to single-handedly smooth this over, isn't he? "Hey, since you're down here—we're going to party on one of the guy's yachts over in Bishop's Landing tonight. You should come."

And look at my sailboat, waiting there at the dock, empty? That's where I took Eva after the poker club. That's where I wanted her in my arms so much I almost lost my mind. "No, thanks."

Zach scoffs. "You used to be a good time. What happened?"

I glare at him. He's an asshole. He doesn't know anything.

And I'm making it worse, because I *know* that. I know that Zach's family is doing all right. I can see from the set of his jaw that he realizes he's fucked up with his boss.

"He's settling down," one of the other guys pipes up. "You're engaged, right, Finn? He's probably going to have a shit ton of babies."

They all laugh.

It's a good joke, isn't it? Me, settling down and having babies. Me, ruining Eva's life. Me, with seven years left to go on the clock before I'm not *me* anymore.

Matt steps in and puts a hand on my shoulder. "Come on. One last hurrah? It'll be fun."

Zach echoes him, and then they press in. *One last time. One more time, Finn.*

It hurts. I'm facing down years of *last times.* I'll never attend another first baby appointment with Eva. That was one of them, and it's gone.

"You know what? Fuck it. I'll go."

They all cheer.

One last hurrah.

CHAPTER FIFTEEN

Finn

T HE WAVES IN the bay by Bishop's Landing are choppy tonight. They slosh against the dock pilings and the side of the yacht.

Nobody hears them now.

Lights blaze from all the windows, casting a drunken glow on the waves. That's all I'd see if I looked out.

I stopped looking hours ago.

Music blares from a set of speakers behind the fully stocked bar. I had one shot when I first arrived. Didn't need any more.

Zach slaps my shoulder, harder this time. He's drunk as hell and still beating me at pool.

"You're shit-faced," I shout at him over the music. "How the hell do you keep winning?"

"I'm an expert at pool," he shouts back.

Whisky spills over the top of his glass.

Women in short dresses circle us, leaning in to show off their cleavage. It's wall-to-wall rich assholes in here. Pure debauchery.

None of it touches me.

It's a feat, because this place is packed with people. They sprawl on all the available furniture. Most of them are high or drunk or fucking.

I don't want to fuck someone in one of the staterooms, or on the curved leather sofa, like the couple going at it now. I don't want to get high. And I don't want to jump off the side of the yacht into black water.

It's hot and loud and exactly the kind of scene I spent years seeking out. I drowned myself in these places before. Escaped from my head.

I lose another three hundred dollars to Zach.

He gets pulled away by two women and re-placed by a guy I don't know. He takes Zach's pool cue, bets me four hundred, and we play.

Can't keep my mind on the shots. There are too many bodies in the room. Too much heat. It's a large yacht, though not as big as mine. Still not enough room.

It's not safe.

The guys were right. I'm not a good time anymore, and it's because I can't help noticing

how dangerous this is. It's not *likely* that there will
be an emergency on the yacht, but if there is,
there's going to be a crush of people. Somebody
could get hurt.

They're already in danger from the sheer
amount of drugs and alcohol. An overdose isn't
out of the question. And nobody's looking out for
each other at this point in the evening. People will
take advantage.

Another game of pool. Another loss. Six hundred this time. At least two thousand dollars of
my money is in other people's pockets.

It was always this dangerous.

The realization comes on slow.

I was in danger at these parties, too. I was in
danger when I drove fast cars without any regard
for the speed limit. I was in danger every time I
visited the underground casino.

It didn't matter.

My future trapped me, but it also *freed* me. I
could take any risk I wanted. I could sit at the
illegal poker table until the cops were bursting
through the door. I could go to illicit boxing
matches on nights when the crowd was blood-
thirsty and out of line. I could drive as fast as I
wanted, turning out the headlights to speed
through black nights.

Because it would be almost a blessing if I died that way. *Any* way, before the ugly, lonely end.

"I might have a death wish," I muse to the guys at the pool table.

One of them blinks at me. "You're just terrible at pool."

I'm not even trying. Am I trying in my life, or am I just pretending? Either way, Eva doesn't need me. She's a better parent than ten thousand men and women put together.

In fact, she has everything. Wealth. Ability. A sound mind.

Finn: *I'm sorry.*

She doesn't answer my text.

I abandon the pool table and push into the crowd. Eddies of people suck me in to dance. My body moves mindlessly, swaying for long enough that they spit me back out again. None of them smell right. None of them *is* right. None of them is the brave, beautiful Eva Morelli, who deserves so much more than I can give her.

Half of me is searching for her on the yacht. I reach for her in every tight clutch of people, my palms looking for the particular curve of her hips. The fall of her black hair. *I won't abandon you, Finn. Not for anything.*

"I'm nothing but pain."

"You're *hot*." A blonde woman looms in close, a strobe light flashing on her face, champagne spilling from her glass. "Let's find someplace where we can be alone."

I laugh at her, and she ignores me.

I didn't want Eva to ignore me. I wanted her to look at me with those huge, dark eyes and never stop.

Well, I should have been careful what I wished for. She saw past the playboy shell. Oh, she loved visiting the underground poker club. Eva got a rush from betting on an underdog. But she knew. She saw what I was trying to hide.

That I'll break her heart every day until I'm dead.

"Finn," someone calls.

Yes, I proposed. But it wasn't real. It wasn't how she wanted it to be. The proposal hurt her as much as telling her I didn't care. The truth is that I don't really want it. I don't want her shackled to me by a wedding band. I don't want her to see me drooling and senseless and afraid.

Fuck, I'm so scared.

It's a broken champagne glass through my heart. Jagged glass. I put a hand to my chest and stumble out onto the deck of the yacht. Cool

TWO FOR THE SHOW

evening air makes it easier to breathe, but what's the point?

What good does it do anyone, least of all me?

Eva doesn't have to go down like this. She can be like my mother. It hurt when she left. I won't pretend it didn't. I spent a long time raging at her, if only in my thoughts. She found some happiness for herself, though. Some peace. That's not on offer at home. Daniel Hughes doesn't know who he is, more often than not. He doesn't know who *we* are. His confusion makes him violent and unpredictable.

An image flashes into my mind. Eva, stoic despite her fear, her gorgeous mouth set in a firm line as she tries to fend me off. A boy with her hair and my eyes hanging back, watching his father attack his mother. I barely have to work to imagine it. I saw it happen at my own dinner table.

I could be sick.

Still no answer.

No son of Eva's would let her face me alone. He'd be part of her family, too, for as long as she was in her right mind. And she has a family who won't fuck off to Switzerland at the first sign of trouble. The Morellis have their problems. They sure as hell do. They're all wrapped up in each other. Demanding too much from one another. Running hot.

I won't abandon you, Finn. Not for anything.

She learned that loyalty from somewhere. I wish it could have been from me and not from surviving the tyrant reign of Bryant Morelli. But she had to know it before she could give it to me.

Try to give it to me. I can't accept. It'd be the same thing as locking my hand around her ankle and pulling her underwater. It would be okay if I died a few years early. It would be a goddamn tragedy for Eva to spend a single day less on earth.

I barely had anything to drink but somehow I've ended up at the railing, my stomach in knots.

She doesn't know what she's asking me to do. She has no idea how it'll feel to deal with my diapers and watch me stop loving her.

You wouldn't ever stop.

"You're full of shit." The voice in my head doesn't know. Does my father still love my mother? Sure. For thirty seconds a day, when he forgets that she left him. Soon it'll be twenty seconds a day, then ten, then none.

Somebody runs into me.

Eva: *I know.*

Zach, with three of the guys from the office.

He slings an arm around my shoulders and shakes. "There's no fucking way you're seasick. We're not even moving. Did you have too much fun?"

"Way too much." I'm basically sober at this point. Doesn't matter. I feel like hell. Goose bumps pull at my arm hairs.

"Wanna have some more?" His mouth is a white cut in the night. The party's all over the deck. Two guys collide with the railing further down. One of them is trying to fuck the other one. His pants are in the way.

"You want to win more of my money at the pool table?"

"Hell no. Let's race the boats to the north side."

It's a bad idea under any circumstance. The north point of Bishop's Landing is rocky as hell and takes concentration to navigate when it's broad daylight. It's the middle of the goddamn night.

But my mind latches on to the word *race*. It sounds like reckless speed and it feels like an adrenaline rush. It *is* an adrenaline rush. Clears my head.

"You're too drunk to race."

Zach shakes his head. "I'm not. I sobered up.

And I need to work off some of this energy."

The rest of the guys behind him lean in, buzz-ing with anticipation. They're wearing drunk, wide grins. They want me to go with them.

I used to chase this feeling every night. It was the only way I could feel alive. It was the only way to flirt with death. That's what I was doing, wasn't I? Flirting with the idea of being dead. Giving it a kiss on the cheek, even if I couldn't go quite yet. A final thrill. A *last hurrah.* Then darkness.

It sounds so good.

"Why the hell not? I'll even take my boat."

Zach thrusts both fists in the air and cheers. Then they're pushing through the party, getting off the yacht, sprinting down the docks. We end up with more people by the time we're at the sailboats.

I corral four of them into a ragtag crew and climb onto the deck of my fifty-foot bluewater sailing yacht.

My feet land in the spot where I held Eva in my arms. She looked up at the stars. *Beautiful.*

I was looking at her. I couldn't take my eyes off her. *Beautiful,* I'd said. To hell with the stars. All I wanted was to drink her in. *We can pretend,* I suggested.

She could pretend to be mine.

I was fooling myself. I never wanted to pretend. I wanted it to be real, and it couldn't be. My life is a sham that will end in more secrecy and shame.

But damn it, *she* was real.

The other guys are getting themselves together. Two of them are on the dock, yelling at Zach and throwing lines onto the boat.

"We're not letting those bastards win."

"Hell, no," one of my guys shouts. At least one of them has sailed before. I lose myself in getting the boat ready to go. Getting it safely out of the docks so we can rush toward a rocky, dangerous turn. It's easier than thinking of how I've disappointed Eva. It's easier by *far* than thinking about becoming my father. The moments when he recognizes my mother again hurt the worst. All anyone wants is for those times to last, and they never do.

My mainsail swings into place and the wind catches it. Somebody lets out a *whoop*. We're rushing through pitch-black water. Lights from the marina and the party yacht ripple on the surface and fall behind us.

"Faster. *Shit*." One of the guys wraps his arm around my shoulder and points. "They're getting away from us."

They're drunk, and they're not being careful.

I'm done being careful, too.

"Not for long," I tell him.

I'm going to die on the boat that I first kissed Eva Morelli on. I'll die on the boat where I held her and asked her to pretend with me. Where I handed over my heart before I knew what I was doing.

What a way to go.

Chapter Sixteen

Finn

SURPRISE—I'M NOT DEAD.

What I am is cold and wet and miserable. Lockup at the Bishop's Landing police station blows just as much as any other jail. Funny that they haven't added any ritzy touches. It's cinder blocks and a hard metal bench for me.

The boat race did not end in the pleasant darkness I was going for tonight. I didn't even crash my boat. I'm a competent sailor.

Zach and the rest of the guys weren't. They were drunk and high and useless, and they ran into the rocks halfway through the turn. The boat turned over. My sober, fully clothed ass jumped in to pull them out before they drowned.

A capsized sailboat and a bunch of guys shouting at each other in the middle of the night were enough commotion to summon the coast guard. They zoomed into the situation on their rescue boat and started arresting people.

Some of the men scattered. I could've run, but I stayed to make sure they were all alive. Nine of us went out and all nine came back. Zach inhaled so much water that they took him to the back of an ambulance to have paramedics look him over. Everybody else was fine. Just drunk. About half of us got arrested in the end, including me.

The wet clothes are making my skin crawl. There's nothing in the holding cell to dry off with. I've created a puddle of ocean water around my shoes.

This is not one of my finer moments in life.

I'm in lockup, which is the perfect time to realize that I want to be a father. I want the baby. Is it selfish to want a baby who's cursed? Or is it selfish to wish the baby had never come at all? It doesn't matter, anyways. The morality of it. It doesn't matter, because either way I want the baby.

It took getting thrown in jail to realize it.

Heavy footsteps come down the hall. Keys rattle in the lock. The bars screech.

"What were you thinking, Phineas?" Hemingway saunters into the cell, a stern expression on his face. He's doing an impression of me. It would be funny if I weren't so miserable. "It's dangerous to sail at night. And illegal, if you're under the influence."

I rub my frozen hands over my face. It doesn't help. "I wasn't under the influence."

He arches an eyebrow at me. "Is that what the breathalyzer will say?"

"Shut the hell up, Hem. And yes. That's what it said."

"You know we have to discuss this, Finn. This behavior is reckless. You could have been hurt."

"Please. I wasn't hurt. This is funny, but—"

"I'm *worried* about you." The corner of his mouth twitches. He's walking a fine line between humor and sincerity. My brother's probably relishing the fact that I'm the one who fucked up this time. "Running afoul of the authorities isn't like you. If you need to talk, I'm here."

I can't even muster a glare. "At least you came alone."

At least our mother isn't here with us.

"No, I didn't. I'm seventeen. Nobody was going to let me bail you out."

"Jesus fucking Christ, Hemingway, tell me you did *not* bring Mom."

He gives me a slow shake of his head. "Nope."

Quick footsteps echo down the hall, and Eva steps into view. Her head is turned. "Yes, thank you." She's talking to one of the cops, presumably. My breath catches. She's beautiful. A queen, even at three in the morning. Sleek, dark clothes. Her purse in her hand.

She turns to look at me, and I want to slide down to the floor and disappear.

I'm a grown man, so I sit up straight and meet her eyes.

Eva lets out a breath, her mouth a soft curve. I'm sure Hemingway got her out of bed to come here. An irritated flush to her cheeks would be normal. I'd deserve it. I'd deserve a terse, thin-lipped greeting. I'd deserve for her to tell me off.

Eva Honorata Morelli is always going to be more than I deserve. She takes in my wet clothes and disheveled hair with an even gaze. Compassion, not pity.

"I'm sure you're ready to get out of here." The smile she offers matches her tone. It says *we're in this together.* Embarrassed heat fills my lungs, forcing a deeper breath in my soaked shirt.

What a fucking situation to be in. My shame burrows itself deeper. It's too late, and I'm too tired, to belabor this by telling her all the reasons she should have let me rot in this holding cell until morning.

I get up from the bench. Hemingway leaves first. Eva waits by the door of the cell until I'm through. I collect a manila envelope with my wallet and keys from the cops at the desk.

Outside, the night air makes the cloth of my shirt stick to my skin. I want to blame the closed-throat, tight-chest sensation on the awful experience of having to exist in wet clothes. That's not it. Of course it's not. It's Eva, ushering me and Hemingway to the curb of the sidewalk. Her driver waits in a black SUV.

Hemingway climbs into the third row.

"Here." Eva's holding out a blanket to me. "I thought this might be nice to have."

You're nice to have. You're so nice that I fucked this up.

"Thank you."

Quiet wraps us up like that blanket on the ride back to the Hughes Estate. Hemingway disappears inside as soon as we arrive. I turn to close the door behind Eva and find her leaning in to speak to the driver.

"What are you doing?"

She stands tall and gives him a wave. The SUV pulls away, and Eva takes my arm. "You need a shower and dry clothes."

"I can handle that by myself."

Eva purses her lips, reaching ahead to open the front door. "I've thought about it, and I don't care. I'm coming in with you."

"I'm fine."

"You've been in jail. And you're shivering."

I hadn't noticed. Now that Eva's pointed it out, I feel the tremors moving through my limbs like the chop on the water.

At the door to my bedroom, I stop and face her. "You've done enough tonight, Eva. You should go home. Don't start this now."

"Don't start what?"

"Don't start taking care of me like I deserve it."

She considers me, her eyes luminous in the dim hallway. Then she turns and goes through the door without another word.

I can't breathe. My ribs can't decide whether to squeeze the air out of my lungs or rattle around like a racehorse with a broken leg. A dull throb at my temples feels like a hangover.

Eva's the one to start the shower. She takes the blanket from my clenched fists and tosses it into my hamper. Her fingers fly over the buttons of my shirt. It hits the floor with a wet *slap*, followed by my undershirt. My belt. My pants.

Everything joins the pile.

I step into the shower with aching guilt pinching at my neck and my back and everywhere. "I'll be out in a few minutes."

The shower closes with a near-silent *swoosh* across the tile.

There's a pause, but the bathroom door doesn't open. Clothes hit the floor, nearly soundless. Then the shower door opens again.

Eva lays her hand on my elbow.

My chest collapses. I turn into her arms, pulling her close. My cold hands have to be torture on her soft, warm skin, but Eva loops her hands around the back of my neck and pulls me into a kiss.

The hobbling fear that drove me to that party, that made me race the sailboat, explodes.

Eva holds tighter. I lift her from the floor and pin her to the wall of the shower. She melts into me as if I'm not a cold, despairing fool. Her forehead rests hot against my shoulder. Then her teeth dig in.

I drag my mouth along the side of her neck. What was I thinking, getting in that goddamn boat? What was I thinking, not doing this every second?

Eva lifts my chin and kisses me. My hips rock

into her without permission. Her wet heat banishes the rest of the cold from my muscles. She responds to my grunt by taking me deeper, and then we're together.

We're together.

She's here.

She wouldn't leave.

I let my hands roam over her body. We haven't had enough time, but every curve is familiar to me. Welcoming. Like coming home.

With my lips on her skin, *home* doesn't feel like prison. It doesn't feel like resignation. It's right.

Hot water rushes down my skin and want burns through me like a fever. Eva's pleasure in human form. I glutted myself on superficial pleasures for so long, and for what?

Fucking her, and being warmed through, loosens a knot at the base of my throat. I nip the curve of her shoulder. Lick her there. My chest is going to burst if I don't speak. I have no control over what comes out.

I'm not raising a child in a home where he knows he's not wanted.

"I can't do it."

Eva pulls my face to hers and kisses me. Every stroke pushes a half-breath out of her. It's too late to shut me up. The dam's broken.

"I can't want it," I murmur into her mouth. It's the wrong time to tell her this. The wrong time to confess anything. She's clenching around me. Her face is flushed with pleasure and heat. "I can't, Eva. I'm so sorry. I'm so scared."

She kisses me harder, throwing herself into it. I've just admitted an unbearable thing to her. I've proven that my proposal is bullshit. None of my advantages as a man make up for this failing. Eva rolls her hips against mine. Her fingernails dig in to my shoulders. Her eyes close. I don't know how she can come at a time like this. I don't know how I'm about to follow her over.

Eva tips her forehead against mine. Her breath is a soft curl over my lips. "It's okay. It's going to be okay. Don't let go of me."

That's the last thing she says before pleasure overtakes her.

I don't let go.

Chapter Seventeen

Eva

I COULDN'T LEAVE him alone.

Finn was not okay at the appointment. The way he behaved was not acceptable. I know that. And it's not that I've forgiven him for his attitude about the baby. It's not that I'm planning to give up on protecting our child from a lifetime of hurt.

Sometimes a person is an asshole. And they still need my help.

That's my specialty, coming from the Morelli family.

I wake up in his bed, piled under soft blankets.

From the even sound of his breathing, Finn's still asleep. I probably would be, too, if it weren't for the pinch of hunger in my belly. It makes perfect sense that I also feel queasy and unsettled.

It'll go away once I've had something to eat. Another amazing quirk of being pregnant.

Sliding out from the covers doesn't wake him. Finn's sprawled on the pillow, looking as young as I've ever seen him. My heart tugs toward the urge to tuck him in tighter. He's already covered.

The instinct to protect him makes a certain kind of sense.

As hurt as I've been, and as angry as I've been, I know what I'm looking at. Finn's not the first man I've ever seen at his limit. I know he's up against the wall emotionally.

I pad into the bathroom and brush my teeth. When Hemingway called me last night, I got up and went. A boat accident? Finn in jail? There are things you set aside your arguments for.

And when I saw him on that metal bench, wet and absolutely miserable...

I couldn't leave him.

The cruel irony of all of this is that I still love him. I'm not sure I'll ever stop.

He's still asleep when I pull on a pair of his sleep pants and a long-sleeved shirt, smooth my hair, and close his bedroom door gently behind me.

I need to find something to eat. The fact that I stayed over and slept with him might be awkward, but food is a necessity if I want to avoid throwing up. It's not how I prefer to start the day.

It's early, but I'm prepared to find Finn's brother in the kitchen. I'm even prepared to find his father with one or two of his nurses.

I'm *not* prepared to find his mother.

Geneva Hughes sits in the breakfast nook, morning sun slanting onto the book in front of her. She looks glamorous in a silk robe as she cradles a cup in her hands. Steam rises over the rim.

Hemingway told me she was here, almost in passing. He hadn't wanted to involve her in the jail situation. My pulse speeds up anyway. She's a Hughes now, but she was a Roosevelt. Just like her sister, Caroline, is a Constantine now. I know some of the deepest, darkest secrets of this woman's sister.

Their genetics have clearly contributed to the iconic Constantine look. It's Caroline and Geneva who have white-blonde hair. They have the same aquiline nose, which I've seen on several of Caroline's children. Geneva looks up from her book, and I discover she has the same icy blue eyes as Caroline.

There's something different about her expression. I can't quite put my finger on what it is.

A lack of loathing, perhaps.

"Good morning." She gives me a gentle smile. "You're Eva."

My manners kick into gear, and I cross the room and offer her my hand. "And you're Finn's mother. Mrs. Hughes. Geneva. It's a pleasure to meet you again."

Her hand is soft and cool, like her laugh. "No need for white lies before eight a.m. I know our families are cordial, but Caroline hasn't made it easy. Would you like some coffee? Tea?"

"Tea, please. But I meant it." Geneva's already gliding across the space. She opens a cupboard and pulls out the accouterments for a cup of loose-leaf tea. "I'm glad to meet another member of Finn's family."

She arches an eyebrow at me, her hands moving over the infuser. A kettle of hot water waits on the stove. "My sister's family."

"We can't help who we're born to. I understand it's pretty much the luck of the draw."

Her mouth quirks. "I can see why he likes you."

We take places across from one another in the breakfast nook. It feels outside the realm of possibility that I'd sit down and have tea with Caroline Constantine's sister, but then again, her daughters were at Haley's baby shower.

Which makes me think of my own potential baby shower. My mother and Geneva Hughes making small talk. Me, graciously accepting gifts for the next phase of life, which may or may not actually include Finn.

I sip my tea. The light flavor settles my stomach. "I'm fond of him, too."

"I'd hope so, given that you slept over." Before I can muster a response, Geneva waves a hand. "I don't mind if he brings his lovers to the house. If you want to have meaningless sex, that's fine. Just don't be serious about him."

It's far too late for that. I'm not sure what Finn's mother knows. She probably knows about the engagement, since all of Bishop's Landing does. Her comment tells me she doesn't have any idea about the baby.

In the silence, she studies my face. "Ah. It's clear Finn's told you about his situation."

"Yes. He shared that with me."

"He's a good man."

I wrap both hands around the teacup. The warmth reminds me of the shower last night. Finn's face buried in my neck. *I can't do it, Eva. I'm so sorry. I'm so scared.*

"He is." That's the truth. All I can say, really.

"He's a good man now. He won't always be that way. I hope he was clear about the timeline."

"I've met the older Mr. Hughes. I have some idea of what Finn thinks is coming."

"I mean this kindly, Eva. He doesn't have the first clue of what it's like to watch your husband disappear before your eyes. Worse, actually. He becomes a stranger. A stranger who you've had sex with. A stranger who you've had children with. A stranger who doesn't even recognize you."

I don't want to know. I want to cling to hope.

Doing that would make me a coward.

"Then tell me what it's like."

"It's bloody and violent and heartbreaking. You end up changing the man's diapers. You find him wandering outside, lost, in soiled clothes. A man who would never raise a hand to you slaps you across the face. He forgets he ever loved you. He forgets he knew you at all."

I make a sound of pained sympathy.

"These things start early for the Hughes men." Polite concern edges her voice. It reminds me of her sister until I meet her eyes and find sadness there.

"I think you're trying to warn me away, Mrs. Hughes."

"I'm not trying to warn you. I'm telling you

that you should cut and run."

The directness of her gaze is as sharp as her words. The blunt impact sends a shock through my chest. We're talking about her son. "You're suggesting that I leave him?"

"Yes. You don't need the money. The best thing you can do for yourself and for the baby is to separate yourself from this situation as soon as possible. Have legal documents drawn up that give you full custody and control of your child. You'll need ironclad protection, and you can get it if you start early enough. Go, Eva. And don't look back."

A numb sensation spreads over my face. This isn't the conversation I expected to have at the Hughes's breakfast nook with hot tea warming my hands. Some motherly prodding, maybe. A little light disapproval that I slept here last night.

Nope. She's telling me to wholesale abandon her son.

"To spare myself from seeing him…decline?"

"Not to spare yourself. To *save* yourself. The Hughes legacy isn't the money or the company or the social status. It's this secret. And if you don't leave, it'll kill you."

"You're still here, aren't you, Mom?" Finn's voice, casual and charming, stops my heart.

His mother's eyes slide over to him. Judging by her reddened cheeks, she didn't know he was there. I'm bruised for both of them. For the mother who feels she has to protect other people from her son, and for the son who heard the naked truth from his mother.

Finn straightens up, sticks his hands in his pockets, and crosses the kitchen. He woke up and came to find me. He's all sweatpants and T-shirt and bedhead, and I've still never seen anyone as breathtaking.

Or anyone as determined.

He slides in next to me, the heat of his body meeting mine. I'd feel like I was in his bed again, protected by the sheets, except my face is on fire and my morning sickness is back in full force.

"Eva."

I tear my eyes from the tea cooling in the cup and meet his.

There's no self-conscious tilt to his mouth or embarrassed glance at his mother. Finn looks at me like I'm the only person in the world he could possibly speak to. There's a knot in my throat. What did he think about that suggestion? Did the idea of it hurt him? I don't want that, but I hate even more the idea that he might have liked the idea. That it would be a relief to him if I did that.

"I heard the option she laid out for you. If you really want that kind of life, we can walk out of here and get on the phone with the lawyers. I'll sign any document you ask me to. I'll make sure you and the baby are provided for, and I'll give up my rights. I'll bow out."

Finn got his voice from his father, but he got his calm, assured cadence from Geneva. He's as matter-of-fact as she was.

Almost as matter of fact. An emotion struggles under the surface of his words. He's keeping it in check.

A memory flashes. His face, filled with relief, when Leo came out holding his new baby, safe and sound. Another: Finn in the waiting room of the doctor's office, explaining in the same level tone that he would take care of me no matter what his feelings were. Another: the distress on his features in the light of the ultrasound machine. He wasn't hiding behind charm and distance then.

"But?"

Finn takes my hand, right there on top of the table. "But I don't want that."

Oh God, I don't want it either. Geneva's suggestion felt callous and horrifying. I understand she's trying to spare me from her own pain, but going forward with that plan would be worse than turning my back on Finn. I'd be turning my back on myself. I don't give up on the people I love, even when it's hard. Even when it's awful. Even when it seems like there's no light at the end of the tunnel.

"I thought you didn't want the baby."

"I was wrong." Finn shakes his head like even the memory of his *not wanting* can be shaken out. "I want the baby. I want this baby. *Our* baby. I want to watch him grow up. I want to teach him how to be a man in whatever time I have left. I want him, Eva. And I'm sorry for making you doubt that."

My throat is tight. I've wanted these words from him so much. I've craved them. I thought that if Finn changed his mind, if he wanted this baby, I'd have everything.

But it's not everything, is it? It's not the only thing.

Does he want me, too?

Chapter Eighteen

Finn

MONEY CAN BUY a person out of many, many things.

It can't get me out of shareholder meetings.

The C-Suite begins preparing for them months in advance. We're in a constant state of research, discussion, and presentations. These meetings are the price we pay for being given frankly outrageous tax breaks from the government. They've been the bane of my existence since I signed those Power of Attorney documents at the age of sixteen.

Nobody needs the CEO to weigh in on the minutiae of the day-to-day. It's when we have to tell our shareholders how things are going at Hughes Industries that people notice my dad's absence the most.

This round of presentations happens in the big meeting room—the one that fits the entire executive team. One of our rising stars in accounting gives a fast-paced presentation on the large screen. I have to admire how deep in it he is. The men at the meeting table seem largely forgotten, including me.

"—opportunities for reinvestment. There's enough capital percentage-wise that we should take the temperature of the shareholders to gauge whether they'd prefer stock buybacks, or—"

The CFO is a razor-sharp man named Alex Wong. He raises a hand. "One second, Shawn. What's Mr. Hughes's opinion on next moves? Can we get him on Zoom?"

He directs his question to me. The rest of their heads swivel to watch. The *Mr. Hughes* in question is obviously my father.

"I can tell you," I say, my voice easy. "We talked about it last night at the dinner table. He's not concerned with shareholder opinions. It's just going to lead to a scattershot approach. No, what they want, what they *need,* is leadership. That's why we're going to set an aggressive reinvestment plan."

There's a pause. Wong studies me. "I have a few questions for him about the particulars."

I don't give the awkward silence a chance to breathe. "Fine by me. Send it to him in an email."

I'll be the one to get the email. I'll be the one to answer it on my father's behalf. It's the way of the world until Hemingway takes over.

Shawn the accountant moves to continue. Heads turn back to him.

"No, I'm sorry." Wong looks me in the eye so pointedly that I know he'd rather be looking anywhere else. "I don't appreciate working my ass off for a guy who can't even be bothered to show up to the office."

"This isn't about him," I say, because I'm prepared for comments like this. "Hughes Industries is bigger than one man. My father oversees global strategy. He isn't here to babysit executives."

My C-Suite is exchanging *many* wide-eyed, furtive looks across the table.

This is an uncomfortable turn in the tide. They don't normally hang on for so many rounds.

One of them throws one of those looks to Wong. I can see the courage straighten his back. He won't raise his voice, but pushing the issue like this is a challenge all by itself.

"No, it *is* about him. It's strange that we haven't seen him in so long. It's, what, five months?

Isn't that what we figured out, Barry? We counted it out."

Barry, an older man with set wrinkles that never seem to change, nods. "Five and a half. We used to see him every quarter."

"We used to see him every *day*." This from Nila Kabir, who's been with Hughes Industries even longer than Barry. Christ, this is devolving fast. I need to put a stop to it.

"Might not have been that much." Barry shrugs. He keeps his options open. Always has.

From the other side of the table, a woman named Susan leans forward. "There's no tactful way to say this, Mr. Hughes, but is the elder Mr. Hughes…even alive?"

Bitter irritation leaves an unpleasant aftertaste on my tongue.

It's time to parade my father through the office again. We do it every six months like clockwork.

It's always risky. Sometimes necessary.

With every month that passes, it becomes more unavoidable. It's not like the old days, when Grandpa Hughes could stop by the office for a wave and a smile, then disappear for another six months. Vague excuses worked back then. If I said my dad was on an extended trip to Europe, for instance, people would start looking for proof.

In the days of social media, it *is* strange for someone to be entirely absent. Even someone my dad's age, who was born well before Mark Zuckerberg was a twinkle in the universe's eye.

I'm going to put her in her place, because that's what everyone's waiting for. That's what they need to feel secure—that they're under strong leadership. But in the end, they'll win.

I'll drag my father through here, risking a major episode, to prove he's alive.

I glare at her. "Did you see an obituary, Ms. Dixon? Did you attend his funeral? Did the Dow Jones take a dive? Did the entirety of Hughes Industries roll to a halt while I wasn't looking?"

She looks abashed. "No, sir."

I spread my hands flat on the desk and put on a smile that says I'll humor them, but I'm a bit pressed for time. "My father is alive and well, thank you for asking. He'll be in, of course. And he'll be thrilled to know that you're more concerned over his health than the goddamn investment strategy."

There's murmured assent around the table. It doesn't make me feel much better. A handshake will head off this line of thinking for now. It won't work again. My dad just won't be stable enough.

It's time. Hell, I should have made this move months ago. It was wishful thinking on my part. I hoped we'd be able to get by on a few more years of quarterly visits.

Neither of us has that kind of time. If I push this even another year, I'll be that much closer to my own expiration date. Hemingway needs hands-on experience running the company. I can't bring him in without raising suspicion unless I'm the CEO.

Sweat prickles at my collar. My shirt feels as tight as our timeline. If I only have seven years, we're behind schedule.

Shawn launches back into his presentations. People tap on screens and take notes on legal pads. For the moment, they're not watching me.

It's time for me to officially transition from acting CEO to CEO. Past time, really. It's better for everyone if my dad enters real retirement.

Making the decision feels like jumping off my sailboat into cold water. It clears my head and pumps adrenaline into my system. I'd like to walk it off. I settle for picking up a pen and scrawling some notes on the pad in front of me.

In a way, I'm rescuing both me and my dad from a midnight crash on the rocks. I'm pulling him out before he goes down in a public wreck.

And I'm giving myself as much time as possible to avoid a similar fate. As CEO, I can put policies in place that will make it easier for Hemingway to replace me. We can cut down on the time he'll need to spend coordinating my visits to the office.

But that's not what makes my heart race with anticipation and profound relief.

It's that I can stop pretending.

No more signing emails with my dad's name. No more built-in delays to give the impression that he's being consulted. No more office visits.

One more office visit.

My breath catches in my lungs, sticking until it burns. I always knew I'd arrive at this decision someday. I didn't know I'd feel...

Grief about it.

I put a hand on the front of my jacket and focus on the presentation. I've spent most of my life preparing for this. Daniel Hughes was the one who started the process. His position as CEO hasn't only been part of the show we put on for the employees and shareholders. It's been a sign of hope.

Mine.

I told myself that I was pragmatic. That I don't sweep things under the rug. Ironic to discover it wasn't true.

Keeping up appearances with my dad as CEO

was a front, but it covered up something I'd never admit to anyone—I hoped he'd prove himself wrong.

I hoped that somehow, we'd be able to fight off his decline. Slow it. As long as he was CEO, I could tell myself that it wasn't so bad. As long as he could shake hands at the office, it couldn't possibly be as terrible as he'd feared.

Taking his place means accepting where he's at, and it hurts.

One more office visit. One last hurrah.

It's the right thing to do. It's not fair to put the stress of the visits on him. Not in the state that he's in. I'd just hoped this day wouldn't actually come.

I'd *hoped.*

That's a move straight out of Eva Morelli's playbook.

Maybe we're not so different after all.

The painful pinch in my lungs subsides. Shawn's presentation fades back into view. Clarity returns, along with excitement. With purpose. I'm not going to pretend anymore. I'm not going to wait. Living at the mercy of this disease has been a crushing weight.

It's gone. For a little while, it's gone.

But I'll owe Eva for that forever.

CHAPTER NINETEEN

Eva

NOBODY CAN RESIST the new baby.

I get a front-row seat to the incredible pull Abby has on just about everyone in the family, including me. She's three days old when they come home from the hospital, and four days old when Leo sends me a casual text asking if I can move things around on my schedule and come over.

Haley's sister, Petra, does the same thing. The difference is that she has a toddler of her own and a husband who doesn't seem to like it when she's out of the house.

The day Geneva Hughes tells me to *cut and run,* I get a text ten minutes after leaving the Hughes estate. "Change of plans," I tell my driver. "Take me to Leo's."

Gerard meets me at the front door with tight lines of worry around his eyes. "They're upstairs, Eva."

In the bedroom, Haley leans against a stack of pillows, Abby in her arms and tears running down her cheeks. An anxious, exhausted Leo sits on the edge of the bed, smoothing her hair and agreeing with everything she says.

He looks at me, his eyes shadowed with dark circles. That's all it takes.

"I hope my room is ready," I announce, as brightly and softly as possible. This is a joke. My room at Leo's is always ready. He has the sheets refreshed and the space dusted and cleaned every week, regardless of whether I'm here or not. I go to kiss Haley on the cheek and Abby on the top of her downy head. "I'm too lonely in the city."

Haley turns her huge blue eyes on me. Her chin dimples. "My sister couldn't stay," she manages. "And my mom…"

Her mom has been gone for a long time.

I sit down next to Leo and take Haley's hand. "I don't have anywhere else to be. Now—does anything sound good to you? Something to eat? A movie to watch? Want to tell me every single detail of how weird and painful and a little bit awful this is?"

Haley's laugh sounds like a sob. "No. I'm so happy. It's just that everything hurts and my body feels like someone else's and I don't know what I'm doing."

Later, when Haley's napping, Leo tells me that she ugly-sobbed when Petra left. He holds Abby close, curled on his chest. "She wants a woman to talk to. She loves Mrs. Page, but I pay her to be here. It's not the same."

"What about you? Are you surviving?"

He rubs gently at Abby's back. "I'm up all night checking to see if she's still breathing."

I stay.

The first thing I do is take over scheduling. I let it be known in the family that anyone who wants to visit or check in or request photos should text me first.

They *all* want to come over.

I arrange small groups. Low-pressure visits. My parents and Daphne arrive with a box that turns out to contain Leo's baby blanket. Daphne takes a photo of our dad holding Abby. She's wrapped in the soft blue cloth with its bunny pattern.

"Look," she whispers, showing me the photo on the screen of her Nikon.

It takes my breath away. In the photo, Dad's

looking down at Abby as if the rest of the world doesn't exist. I've only ever seen that expression on my father's face in some of the oldest family pictures.

Our mom holds Abby like an invisible timer is counting down and she doesn't want it to end. Daphne beams at the baby, telling her about paint colors and explaining what an easel is. "Daphne," she says, her voice low and musical. "I'm Daphne. What if you learned to say my name first?"

In the long, quiet stretches between visitors, I help Haley. Leo makes semi-regular excuses to go pretend to work in his office so we can talk. He's never gone for long.

"This is so much harder than I thought it would be," Haley admits one morning.

"Taking care of her?"

"No. Abby's perfect. It's existing that's hard. Sometimes I feel like I'll never be able to sit up by myself again."

"You will," I promise her.

"Oh, look." Haley's voice goes high and awed. "She's yawning. Isn't that the cutest thing you've ever seen?"

"She's a miracle."

Haley's painkillers from the surgery make her tired. Her eyelids are drooping when Leo asks her if there's anything she wants. Anything at all.

Abby's just finished nursing, and Haley lets her head fall back on the pillows. "I want a nap. Do you want to hold her, Eva?"

"Literally always." I take the warm, sleepy bundle from Haley's arms and tuck her against my chest. "We won't go far."

Haley's breathing deep by the time Leo and I reach the bedroom door. He closes it behind us, and his shoulders drop down. "She's better. Right?"

"A little bit better every day."

Leo keeps his hand on my arm all the way down the stairs. I'm carrying precious cargo, after all. We don't have to discuss where we're going. His den is everyone's favorite room in the house. That's because I gave the designers precise instructions for the sofas. More comfortable furniture doesn't exist.

We sit on the one facing the courtyard window. Leo hesitates for a split second before he rests against the cushions and stretches his legs out next to mine on the ottoman. I pat Abby's back. I've made it a point to learn her favorite rhythm. At least, I hope I have.

One of the birds that lives in Leo's courtyard lands on the sill and cocks its head. It gives the glass a light, friendly tap.

"She's sleeping," Leo says. "Don't you dare wake her up."

The bird fluffs its wings and flies away.

"Do you think babies like to swim?" He glances at Abby, who was not woken by the bird. "I do own a heated pool. And the weather's still nice."

"I think babies like to be held in warm water. Swimming, I'm not so sure about."

He rearranges his feet on the ottoman. Cloud shadows dapple the sunlight in his courtyard. The baby sleeps. Even the sound of her breathing is unbearably adorable.

I wonder if Finn will sit with me like this, with our baby asleep in my arms, or if he'll try to keep his distance. *I want the baby* doesn't mean *I want you.*

"You should just tell me what happened instead of brooding," Leo says.

"I'm not brooding."

"One corner of your mouth frowns when you're thinking about something that bothers you. Something like...I don't know. Finn Hughes? You still haven't told me how he proposed."

I let out a sigh. "With a pitch deck."

"Pardon?" Leo's the picture of *what the fuck, Eva?*

"Well, technically, he tried to tell me we were going to get married at Daphne's reception. Then, when I refused, he put together a pitch deck. It was essentially a business proposal. He didn't mean it."

"So you refused again."

I turn my body so I can glare at him without disturbing Abby. "You are *not* judging me for turning him down."

"I would never do that." The surprise in Leo's eyes is instantly replaced with sincerity. "Of course, you don't have to marry him. You're extremely rich and extremely capable of doing whatever you want. It's a little annoying, actually. I'm only good at real estate. You're good at everything."

I scoff at him. "But you think marrying him wouldn't be the worst thing."

Leo's bird lands on the windowsill again. "Being married would have its advantages. Society is old school and puritanical and so are our parents. I wouldn't judge you for considering it, even if he did somehow think it was appropriate to give you a pitch deck instead of a ring."

Abby takes a deep breath, and a heavy feeling

sinks deeper into my bones. Being pregnant is tiring. So is keeping secrets. It's almost always easier to carry them with someone else, and ironically harder *not* to tell Leo.

"There's something else."

"What?"

He shifts, putting his arm across the back of the couch and a bit more distance between us so we can see each other's faces. The way he studies mine says he's already trying to figure out what it is.

"Well...I have to swear you to secrecy."

Leo's eyes widen in teasing shock. "Again? My previous vow was binding in perpetuity."

"I'm serious."

"*I'm* serious. I would never give up your secrets."

"This one's not exactly mine."

He sobers, his eyes traveling down to the baby. "Is it Hughes?"

"The men in his family deal with early-onset dementia."

Leo tilts his chin. "How early?"

"Their thirties."

He looks out the window, and I can see the calculations flashing in his eyes. "Hughes Industries is a family company. Daniel Hughes is in his fifties, isn't he? Younger than Dad. And Finn—"

"They've been hiding it. Finn had Power of Attorney documents that would install him as acting CEO at the first sign of trouble. He took over Hughes Industries when he was sixteen."

Leo's eyes come back to mine. "Shit. *Shit.*" His mouth drops open, then closes again. "How could they have kept such a massive secret from everyone while he's still the CEO?"

"The same way we did. By sticking to our story and making sure people saw what we wanted them to see."

My brother blinks, and his eyes slide to the corner of the room. They're distant for a few heartbeats. Then a shudder moves through his body. He's shaken himself out of the memories.

"Is it bad?"

Geneva's words replay in my mind. *It's bloody and violent and heartbreaking.* Daniel Hughes, shouting, distressed. Finn's face paling at the docks when the call about his father came in.

"Yeah." A knot settles in my throat. "And he's sure the baby is going to be a boy. He's certain he'll have the same disease. Which means it's my concern now, too."

Leo leans against the couch and runs a hand

through his hair. The bird fluffs its feathers in the corner of the window. It taps again. *I'm still here. I'm still here. I'm still here.*

I don't have to spell it out for him. He's already running the scenarios in his head. Another quick breath. Leo puts his arm around my shoulders, careful not to jostle the baby.

"We'll solve this. We have to." It's final. *We have to.*

"Yeah. I think so, too. But the Hughes have ridiculous amounts of money. They could buy and sell entire pharmaceutical companies, and they haven't solved it." Hopelessness I don't want to feel closes around my heart.

Leo runs his palm up and down my arm. "The Hughes have always had money. They didn't have you."

"I'm not a miracle worker."

"That's not true, and you know it. You're the one who found my shirts."

All of Leo's undershirts and sheets and even his rash guards for swimming are made with the softest pima cotton available in the world.

"All I found was the farmer."

"In the middle of nowhere. In *Peru.*"

True. A tiny farm that's contracted with me from now until forever. We pay them three times their operating costs for their exclusivity.

"The shirts were simple. Not easy, but simple."

"It took you a year, Eva. You could have given up after the first ten options didn't work. Or even the first twenty."

I tried thirty other suppliers across the United States, Australia, and South America before I found the farmer in Peru. A fourth-generation tailor in New York City produces all the finished items in addition to fitting Leo's suits.

"It wasn't an option to stop looking. You needed them."

"Yes." Leo can't deny it. He put his hands over his face and cried when the first good sample shirt came in. That's how relieved he was, and how much pain he'd been in. "And my point is, you could have taken the loss."

"And let you keep suffering? No." If the solution existed on the planet, I was going to find it. Or invent it. A long line of doctors hadn't been able to help. In the end, it was a matter of hunting down the correct raw materials. "I couldn't ever give up on you."

Not even in his worst pain and despair. That year was awful. Every other fabric blend I tried was unbearable on his skin. We used different fabric treatments and different manufacturing processes. Nothing worked until we found the right solution.

It must be equally unbearable to live in Finn's head. The curse causes him pain, and if our child is a boy, it'll hurt him, too.

Fixing their suffering won't be as simple as finding the right fibers. Not this time.

"I've never known you to give up on anyone you love, sister mine."

"This might be beyond me. It's medical science, not fabric." My stomach is an empty pit. "And it's so hopeless. It's how he's lived for so long. I'm afraid to disappoint him."

"You won't. You couldn't. We'll solve it together. I'll help you." The first hot tears slide down my cheeks. I wipe them away before they can land on Abby. Leo pulls me close, and I let my head rest on his side. "Don't keep it in. Tears don't mean you're giving up. They mean you're gathering the strength to begin."

CHAPTER TWENTY

Finn

I DON'T JUST owe Eva Morelli for giving me a family and showing me that life doesn't have to be bleak and empty.

I'm also hopelessly in love with her.

I walked out of that meeting and went to meet with the family for dinner.

Admitting it to myself had the same shocking quality as admitting it's time to become the CEO of Hughes Industries. A few moments will pass, and then—*oh my God. I'm in love with her.*

I'm in love with her.

And every second I don't tell her is wasted time. I'll never get it back.

The ring arrives at the Hughes estate. It's exactly what I chose for her.

It's not enough.

Eva would say that wasn't true, but I know better. She wants to be together. She wants to be loved. I can give that to her. I'm going to give that to her.

I text her from the Hughes Industries headquarters as soon as I've sent my secretary home for the day.

> **Finn:** *Do you have plans for the evening?*
> **Eva:** *Why? Did you have something in mind?*
> **Finn:** *If you're free to meet with me, I do.*
> **Eva:** *I could be free.*

I pull up in front of her apartment building a short while later.

> **Finn:** *I'm here.*

No reply. Then she steps into view on the sidewalk. It doesn't look like she came from inside.

I climb out and offer her my hand. "I hope you didn't rush home for me."

Eva tucks a lock of hair behind her ear. "Leo swore they'd be okay."

She's been at her brother's house, helping to take care of the new baby and her parents. It kept Eva busy. It gave me time to come to my goddamn senses about how much I want her in my life.

About how much I want her, period.

"So." She's so beautiful like this. Always. I barely have any sense of her dress because her face is so striking. "What did you have in mind?"

I stick my hand in my pocket and take out the quarter. It's a perfect flip. The coin turns over in the air on its way to Eva's palms.

"How about a bet?"

Her smile lights up her face. The sun's already setting, and its embers reflect in her dark eyes. "What do I get if I win? Foam on my Starbucks order?"

"Come with me and find out."

She sits in the passenger seat and talks to me on the way out of the city. I'm about to leap out of my skin from nerves and anticipation, but her voice soothes me. *You wouldn't believe how good a newborn baby smells, Finn. She's just this little squishy bundle. Yesterday, she tried to lift up her head. I was so proud. It was incredible.*

Eva gets quieter at the city limits of Bishop's Landing. She's silent when I pull the car into a spot near the docks.

I can't read her expression. She looks out at the bluewater sailing yacht. If she's anything like me, a montage of that first night is playing in her head. I feel just like I do now. Desperately glad to be near her. Overwhelmed with hope.

I go around to her door and offer her my hand.

Eva takes it.

She sticks close as we approach the yacht and lets me steady her during the transition from dock to boat.

Then we're standing on the deck, right where we started.

I had a proposal for her then, too. A fake relationship. I offered her a fling. A distraction. And she became the only reality I want.

We've already made a new future together. I want to be part of it. I want her to be everything.

The first stars of the evening are appearing over the last of the sunset. I breathe in the moment. I want to remember this for as long as I can. The fading summer air. Eva's hand in mine. The stars, coming back again, just like they promised.

The two of us, together, facing the future.

Then I turn her to face me. Drink her in with as much attention as I gave the sunset. I want to remember this, too. The flush in her cheeks. Her black hair stirring in the breeze. The soft set of her lips. I run my thumb over the corner of her mouth.

"Since the moment I saw you in your parents' house, I've been trying to convince myself not to love you." Eva's lips part as if to interrupt. "No, this is important. I really tried. I fed myself every justification for why I couldn't be with you. I explained it to myself a hundred different ways. At least ten times a day, I convinced myself that you'd be better off taking your chances with anybody else."

Memorize her. Don't forget.

"But in the end, none of those reasons changed the fact that I love you. That I'm in love with you. I can't stop loving you. It's hopeless. For a long time, everything seemed that way. I told myself there was no point in getting attached. I told myself that it was wrong, in fact, to let anyone get close to me. I wouldn't be able to give them the time they needed."

Eva leans her cheek into my palm.

"But then I saw you standing there with your mother, and I couldn't leave you. I should have taken it as a sign that I'd never be able to walk away. How could I? You're beautiful and strong and you had something I desperately needed."

"What was it?"

"Hope."

"God, Finn. You break my heart, you know that?"

"And you break mine. You didn't want to accept my fatalistic bullshit. I told you I had seven years, and what did you say? You said—*give me seven years. Give me seven months.*"

"I would have taken anything you'd give me."

Past tense. She's speaking in the past tense. "You were telling me that I was enough, even if I didn't have a decade to spend with you. I was a fool. I couldn't hear it then. I couldn't accept your love then."

Her dark eyes shimmer with tears. "What about now?"

My chest feels overfull. What happens next matters too much, but I won't look away from it. I won't avoid it. The fall is coming either way, but I'm going to soar on the way down.

"There's nothing I want more in the world. I don't want to spend my life counting the days. I want to spend every day looking at you. Loving you. Letting you love me back, for exactly as long as we have."

I get down on one knee, and a tear falls down Eva's cheek.

Her hand is in mine, warm and soft. It's home.

Remember. Remember. Remember. I want to remember this even when I have early-onset dementia, even when I'm babbling and out of my mind. It feels impossible that I could forget.

"I should have done this the first time I brought you here. I wanted to. I knew it then, how dangerous you were to me. I shouldn't have wasted a second trying to convince myself otherwise." I pull the box from my pocket and press it into her palm. "I love you, Eva Honorata Morelli. I want to give the rest of my life to you. Will you be my wife?"

She swallows hard, more tears shining in her eyes. "That's what you want?"

"If all you were willing to offer me was scraps, then I'd happily take those. And that's all I deserve. I know that, too. But I desperately want to marry you."

"Yes," she whispers. "Yes. I will. I'll marry you."

I'm quick to take her into my arms and kiss her, but she's already crying. Happy tears. Eva wipes them away while I open the ring box. She gasps at the sight and starts to cry again.

Her hand trembles when she holds it out to me.

"This is one of the greatest honors of my life,"

I tell her. *Remember.* And then I slip the ring onto her finger. It's an antique in the Hughes family. Priceless, but it means nothing without the warmth of her body. *Remember, goddamn it. Don't forget.*

There's a moment of stillness. We both look at the ring. A tangible sign of a real relationship. Nothing fake about it. Nothing pretend. Nothing transient. This ring means forever.

Then her arms go around my neck and her mouth is on mine and she said yes, she said yes, she loves me.

I need her so much. Her need matches mine. I take her down to thick blankets stretched across the deck and prop myself over her and let myself look.

Remember.

I wanted this that first night, too.

"I remember you like this," Eva breathes. "You were over me. You were surrounded by stars, but I couldn't see them. I could only see your eyes. Nothing but you."

"I'm never going to forget you like this, Eva. I swear to God."

She's beautiful in the warmth of the sunset. My ring on her finger. Our baby in her belly. She's going to be my wife. There's nothing that could be better than this.

"You look so happy," she murmurs, tracing a finger over my cheekbone. "Not the way you were before, though. Not laughing or teasing or charming the panties off women everywhere. That seemed happy, but underneath it felt like something else. Something manic."

"That wasn't real. This is. This is true happiness, darling."

My wife.

Then I can't stand to be separated from her. Not for another moment. I pull her out of her clothes. Eva does the same to me. She pulls me down over her.

I'm free to feel her skin against mine. Free to press kisses to her collarbone, and lower. This is what I wanted to do that first night. I wanted to worship her, and I didn't. I held back. I told myself it could wait.

I'm never going to do that again.

I kiss her everywhere I can reach while she arches underneath me. No project is more important than memorizing all her soft places. All her curves. Eva shivers under my touch, begging, and when I push myself inside her, she cries out.

I don't care. Let everyone hear how much she loves this. How much she loves me.

For the first time, there's no fear between us. I feel like a different person and the one I was always meant to be. I've spent years searching for a sense of peace, and I've found it.

Eva holds me close and lets me watch her take her pleasure in my body. It's a gorgeous sight. She shakes out her heat over me.

"Let me see you," she demands, her voice sweet. Her hands on my face keep me in view. "God, Finn. You're everything I need. It was so hard to pretend I didn't want you."

"Don't pretend, Eva. Tell me every day. I'm going to insist on it."

I don't have to hold myself back. I let my pleasure have its way until I'm pulsing inside her. Eva's body moves with mine like she's meant for me.

She is.

She rolls us over before I've finished and the sway of her hips keeps me hard. So hard that I have no choice but to come for her again. Eva balances herself on my chest, holding on with her nails, and takes every last bit of pleasure she can find.

When it releases us, she leans down to kiss the fingernail marks she left.

"Don't kiss them too much."

"Why?"

"Because I want them to stay forever."

"Oh, I doubt they will. But I can always make new ones."

I catch her chin in my hands and pull her close so I can see this word, this promise, on her lips. "Always?"

"Always." It's a promise and a declaration of wild, untamable hope. I'm going to feel that with her. I'm going to feel everything with her. Not because I think the curse is broken. Not because I really think I'll make it to the age of forty with my mind intact. But because I'm willing to live as if it could happen, if it means having even a few years with Eva. I'll give her seven years. Or maybe only seven months. And when I'm lost to the world, when I leave her in mind, if not in body, she'll forgive me.

"Kiss me again," I murmur.

Eva leans down, her hair falling over my face, and gives me just what I want.

She gives me so much more.

CHAPTER TWENTY-ONE

Finn

THERE'S ONE FINAL step to take before my life with Eva begins—my dad's last meeting at Hughes Industries. His official goodbye. His retirement, to the public at least.

I plan it carefully, the way I've done everything carefully for years. Even though all I want to think about is my ring on Eva's finger and the future we have together.

I'm finished putting a number of years on it.

I'm not naïve enough to forget the past, but I don't have to let it darken everything.

My dad sits quietly in the second row of the SUV, reading a well-worn copy of *Time* magazine. It's from the last year he worked, truly worked. Sometimes he slips back into a childhood state. Other times he knows we're in the present. But mostly he lives in that last year forever. He likes reading the magazines. They feel new to him, even if they're a decade old.

The driver up front has the music on low. An hour from now, I'll be the new CEO of Hughes Industries. I can focus on his care without forcing him to visit as a charade.

"How are you feeling about going into the office?"

"Hmm?" He doesn't look up from his magazine.

"Some of the high-performers at Hughes Industries are waiting at headquarters to congratulate you on a job well done. They've arranged a cake, and they'd like to shake your hand."

"Oh, I'm sure I can give them that." His smile is an echo of the one he used to wear in the office before his episodes began. My dad loved his work. He liked the energy of the company. That's been hard for him to live without, but he chose this isolated existence.

He chose it back when he was still coherent enough to make choices.

Of course I've watched him age at home. The wrinkles and gray hair have come over time, as he wears pajamas and comfortable clothes around the house. Clothes he can't hurt himself in.

The changes are more marked when he's in a suit.

He still looked like a virile, active, middle-aged man when the curse hit him. His mind was gone, but his body looked strong. Now his body doesn't look strong. He looks old.

"We'll head up to the meeting room first thing. I'll be right there with you. Don't worry about remembering everybody's names. Don't worry about anything."

Dad raises his eyebrows. "You nervous, Phineas?"

"Of course not."

"Good. I know every person there. That's the mark of a leader, you know. It's not just about clocking in and out. Not about paperwork. It's about people. You have to know what makes them tick. I know where every person in that office was born. Who their family is. What they want most in life."

My stomach is in knots when the SUV pulls up to the curb outside the headquarters. Dad abandons his magazine on the seat and hops out onto the curb. The confidence in his stride looks real.

It *is* real.

He thinks he's going to work. His mind has

slipped back into the old, familiar pattern.

"Keep up, Phineas," he calls, though I'm right beside him. "Lots to do today."

I force a laugh. "We're having a light day. Only a celebration."

"Sure, sure. Then I'll need to spend some time at my desk. My three o'clock gets testy if he's kept waiting. We don't get days off, Phineas. Not when our employees are hard at work. It's important to set a good example. We're only as strong as our weakest link."

This is a mistake, a small voice whispers in the back of my mind. Dad's getting attached to the idea of this fictional workday. It's anyone's guess whether he'll forget it once we get to the retirement celebration or double down on the three o'clock meeting that doesn't exist.

He steps into the elevator. If I'm going to stop it, now's the time. It's on the tip of my tongue to remember another meeting we need to attend elsewhere and take him home.

Dad puts his hand out to block the elevator door. "Can't keep them waiting, Son."

I follow him in.

The retirement party is made up of a carefully curated group of attendees. All the C-Suite members. CIO, CMO, CFO. An endless alphabet of them. There are also the most dedicated administrative assistants. Managers and members of other departments who've had personal experience working with Dad or who've helped push the company forward in a big way.

I spot Kevin in the crowd. Kevin, whose youngest daughter graduated from college. My father would have known a detail like that. Now he wouldn't even know Kevin's name.

Everyone breaks into applause as Dad and I step into the spacious room on the executive level.

Confusion flashes through his dark eyes, but he covers it with a grin. "Please. That's enough. Thank you, everyone. You're the ones who make this possible."

I put a hand on his arm and raise my voice. "My father, Daniel Hughes, is the reason we're here. The work we've done at Hughes Industries has changed lives all over the world, but none of it would have been possible without his vision, his work ethic, his knowledge. He taught me what it means to stay committed to a cause that matters, and I can say without a doubt that our work matters."

The CFO comes forward and places a box in my hand.

"Dad, on behalf of everyone at Hughes Industries, I'd like to thank you for everything you did for us. Your performance set a high bar. I think we can all agree that nobody deserves to enjoy retirement more than you." I embrace him and press the box into his hand. "Something to remember us by."

Warm applause fills the room. My dad grins down at the box and blinks away the sheen from his eyes. "This is too much. I haven't even gotten started."

The people nearest to us laugh.

A frown tugs at the corner of his mouth. He wasn't joking. He's wondering why they're laughing.

"You did an incredible job, Dad," I say, trying to wrest his attention away.

"That's right," the CIO says, a middle-aged woman who was just a pencil pusher when dad was still himself. She offers his hand for my dad to shake. "It was an honor to work with you, Mr. Hughes. I hope you give retirement your all as well. I'm talking beach vacations and the best golf in the world."

My dad clasps his hand. He doesn't recognize her. His smile is too wide. It's not real. "I will."

He turns away from the conversation and is faced with another person, hand extended.

I hold my breath.

"Congratulations, Mr. Hughes. Wishing you the best. We'll miss you around the office."

My dad's muscle memory seems to take over. He shakes the man's hand. "You won't have time to miss me. I need to get back upstairs after the party."

"You're a company man at heart, aren't you?" I put my hand on his shoulder and give the man a grin. He smiles back, accepting the joke.

"Always have been," Dad says. "Always will be."

Everyone wants to say a few words, so they step forward in turn.

I wish we could have had this party before his mind began to deteriorate. My regret is an ache clamped around my chest like my dad's hand around the box. He deserved to be recognized for his work, for real. The secret we're keeping stole that from him.

The box holds a gold watch. He hasn't opened the top. I'm not sure he's aware of holding it.

A woman from the marketing department takes his elbow and guides him to the cake. Dad exclaims over it, but when she tries to give him the first slice, he shakes his head. "I won't be sharp for my three o'clock meeting if I'm full of sugar."

"You sure, Dad? You only have one retirement party."

Fifteen minutes. That's how long it'll take everybody else to shake his hand if nobody starts a long conversation.

Fifteen minutes, and I can breathe again.

The well-wishes keep coming.

I bet you're looking forward to your golden years.

Take advantage of your newfound free time and travel. I hear Italy's magic.

Play as much golf as you want. You deserve it. If you ever need someone to drive the cart—

"I'll give you a call," Dad promises.

He won't.

I've always looked up to you, Mr. Hughes.

My father's proud that I work for a company like yours. I'm glad I got the chance to shake your hand.

"I'd be nothing without my team," Dad says over another handshake. His team is down to me, Hemingway, and his nurses now. "It's hard work, but it's worth it."

The man he's speaking to blinks, but doesn't ask Dad to clarify.

Time to wrap things up.

I put a hand on his shoulder. "It's about time

we headed out, Dad. Don't you think?"

He nods, turning toward me. I open my mouth to say our goodbyes.

They don't make it out, because the CFO angles in and shakes my dad's hand. Alex Wong doesn't miss a thing, which is why it's great to have him in that role. It's also the reason why I want to keep him far away from my father.

They've only ever met at fake, staged meetings like this one, only ever shook hands and waved as he did a walkthrough under my supervision. But he's conversed with my father over email plenty of times, in depth emails that discussed confidential, complex financial matters.

"Mr. Hughes. Before you go, I wanted to get your take on the reinvestment strategy for next quarter. Seems important that we're all on the same page."

"We are. Of course we are. That's what makes us an effective team."

"I'm in total agreement. The specific strategy, though. I sent you my thoughts, but I know you disagree on the dividends. We've gone back and forth a few times, but I thought maybe we could talk in person."

Dad frowns, pulling slightly away. He clutches the watch box with both hands.

"I can take it from here, Dad." I meet the CFO's eyes. "We'll discuss the strategy next week. I'm the CEO starting at the open of business on Monday."

"Of course. I mean no disrespect. Your leadership isn't in question." Wong refocuses on my dad. "It's just that your father has one of the best financial minds I've ever had the pleasure of working with. Even though we only talk over email, I've learned so much."

"What happens at the open of business?" It's as if Dad has completely forgotten about Alex Wong. "Phineas. Is there something you're not telling me?"

Wong's brow furrows. "Sir?"

"What's happening Monday?" he demands.

"Dad, let's talk about this outside."

Wong glances at me, suspicious now. I want to cover his mouth with my hand. I want to drag him out of here by his collar. "Didn't you sign off on that? The board voted on it. Unanimous agreement. You voted by proxy. Are you saying that you don't know?"

"Young man." My dad's face is flushing. "I have been the head of this company for ten years."

Fuck.

"Dad, we should go. Everybody needs to get

back to work. You've got appointments on your schedule."

"Ten years?" Wong repeats.

Other people are beginning to listen in. He's been the official CEO of Hughes Industries for more than three decades, not one. This is going off the rails.

"That's right. And I have no plans to step down. I'll be in my office on Monday. If you've got a problem, you can bring it directly to me. Make an appointment with my secretary."

The silence in the room is as thick as the tension.

I keep a calm smile firmly in place. "He's having cold feet at the last minute. The prospect of all those beach vacations and endless golf holes don't appeal to someone as industrious as my dad."

There's confusion in everyone's eyes.

They're wondering if it's a power struggle. And it is, but not a power struggle between father and son. It's a power struggle between the Hughes men and our curse.

And right now, as sweat beads on my forehead, the curse is winning.

My father meets my eyes. "What's going on? Where's Geneva? Where am I?"

"He's not feeling well," I tell everyone. "I should have rescheduled the party. I'm sorry. It's my fault."

"Mr. Hughes—"

Dad whips his head toward Wong. He takes a shaky breath and then steps back.

"Why does it say *retirement* on the sign?" He glances down, discovers the box in his hands, and hurls it to the floor like it burned him. "I'm not retiring. I'm not old enough for that. I have work to do. I wasn't finished. Where is my secretary?" His eyes search the room. "Where is my *office?*"

"What's going on here?" Wong asks. "Is this some kind of episode?"

Yes. That's what I'll say. I'll pretend to be shocked and horrified.

I don't have to pretend to be worried sick.

But then…

"I just dealt with this with my Dad." A woman's voice. "Alzheimer's. Or dementia. Mr. Hughes—"

She tries to move forward, but my dad startles back.

"How long has he been like this?" The CFO asks, his voice sharp with blame. "How long, Finn?"

He's still thinking this is some kind of hostile

takeover.

He has no idea that my dad wanted this. He asked for it to happen this way to preserve his dignity, but it's not working. *It's not working.*

"I'm late for my meeting," my father snaps. His eyes pass over me like I'm one of the strangers in the crowd. "I don't know who the hell you people are. My son is supposed to be here. *Phineas.* Where the hell is he? *What did you people do with him?*"

CHAPTER TWENTY-TWO

Eva

THE DIRECTOR OF the charity benefiting LGBTQ+ youth faces me across my desk, her chin held high, expression stoic. Her eyes reveal the truth. She badly wants this grant. And I want to give it to her. I always did, even before, but I've seen too many millions squandered in administrative costs and never-finished projects to hand it out without due diligence.

I flip the last page on her completely reworked presentation and meet her eyes.

This is one of the best moments in my job. Telling people we're about to change their lives. And the lives of so many more people that the charity helps.

Even sweeter that I get to do it with Finn's ring on my finger.

"I'm impressed. You brought me all the information I asked for and then some." I rise from my seat and offer her my hand. "I'm looking forward to working together on your project."

She clasps my hand, no longer attempting to hide her nerves. "Oh my God, thank you. This is amazing. You have no idea how much this means to us."

"Thank *you*. It's your work that made the difference here."

"I—" She releases my hand and covers her mouth. "I don't want to be rude, but I have to tell my team."

"Go," I say with a laugh. "You deserve a celebratory phone call."

The director heads out of my office, through the waiting area, and into the main corridor at Morelli Holdings. I'm glad we held the meeting here. It's grander than my office at home, and she deserves to feel like she won big.

Except she didn't win it. She earned it.

I'm still basking in her joy when Leo sticks his head in the door. "You ready?"

"I was born ready."

The reason I held the meeting in the official Morelli Fund offices is because there's one other item on my agenda for the day—a meeting with my brothers.

Lucian's the CEO of Morelli Holdings. The Morelli Fund is an arm of the family company, and I manage a growing amount of charitable donations every year. Leo's operations at his real estate firm, the Morelli Property Group, are entirely his own, but the legal structure makes his business a subsidiary of Morelli Holdings.

Together, the three of us are in charge of the family's business and philanthropic interests. We have regular meetings to keep each other updated.

This is Leo's first trip back to the city after Abby's birth. He described it to me as a *test run.* He'll still be on paternity leave for at least the next few months.

"How's Haley? How's my favorite niece?" I ask him on the way up to Lucian's office.

"Petra came to be with Haley while I'm at the meeting. Everyone was happy when I left. Abby slept for four straight hours last night, so Haley has a new lease on life."

I nudge him with my elbow. "What about you?"

"I've already texted her three times asking for pictures. Do you know what she said?" Leo pulls out his phone and reads off the screen. "*You're only going to be gone a few hours, and then you can hold her the rest of the day and night. I promise, she's fine!!!"* He gives me wide, skeptical eyes. "Can you believe that? My own wife."

"You're too much."

"I'm your favorite person, sister mine."

"You're up there." We go into Lucian's office and take seats at his desk.

He looks at us with narrowed eyes, his desk phone pressed to his ear. "No. Stop talking. My next meeting is here. I'll send you an email." The phone clatters into its cradle.

"That was a little rude, Lucian," I point out.

"You know what's rude? Having to hear about Finn's proposal from *this* asshole." He inclines his head at Leo, who rolls his eyes.

"You were there when we announced our engagement. Don't be ridiculous."

His dark eyes glitter. I never told Lucian the engagement was fake. Outside of me and Finn, only Haley and Leo knew.

I might have been wrong. Lucian doesn't miss much.

"Ah, but you didn't have a ring. Odd that Hughes would wait so long to get down on one knee on some rickety dock and put it on your finger."

"He got down on one knee on his sailing

yacht, for the record."

"And you didn't so much as send me a text. Let's see it." Lucian stands up, and I have no idea why.

"See what?"

"The *ring,* Eva. Let us see."

"I've already seen it," Leo teases. "You should have been more persistent."

"Shut your mouth, brother mine. I'm not above shutting it for you."

A strange, pleased warmth suffuses me. I'm often at the center of the family, but I'm not usually the center of attention. I'm not sure I ever allowed myself to imagine showing off my new engagement ring. Certainly not to Lucian.

I get up anyway, unable to stop myself from smiling, my eyes hot with happy tears. Leo stands up, too. I extend my hand over Lucian's desk. He takes it carefully in both of his and examines the ring. Leo leans over and looks, too, though of course he was one of the first people to see.

It's a beautiful ring, a dark gold with a four-carat marquise diamond. Finn offered to buy me a ring, anything I wanted. This one is beautiful, full of history and family.

"Do you like it?" Lucian asks softly. My chest goes tight. He's trying so hard. It's so unlike the

Lucian I used to know as a child.

"I love it."

"What about Hughes?" He looks into my eyes, my hand still in his. "You love him, too?"

I can only nod.

"Good. That makes things easier for me."

"Because you don't have to kill him?"

"Exactly."

"The two of you have to stop threatening people with murder."

Lucian laughs, and the three of us take our seats. "You should be grateful you have brothers who would kill for you. Some people aren't so lucky. Now. Tell me the top-line items from the Morelli Fund."

Honestly, I couldn't have imagined a meeting like this before Lucian took over as CEO. Our father used an iron-fist style of management. He and Lucian butted heads over how to run the company, and they kept everybody at a distance. Lucian was always cold. Always kept himself apart, even when we were kids.

Lucian's trying something different. He insists it's about making the most money, but I suspect that falling in love with Elaine gave him a change of heart. He's not nearly such an aloof bastard anymore. I think part of him was afraid that the rest of us wouldn't accept him back into the fold. Silly. He's a Morelli. There's no keeping him out. The meetings are just one of the ways he shows up for us now.

The meeting runs long. It's just past five when the three of us exit Lucian's office and make our way to the main entrance of Morelli Holdings.

"Elaine wants to come see the baby," Lucian says. "Is she free this evening?"

"You could at least pretend to care that I still exist." Leo's tone is only a little sarcastic.

"Oh, but I do. Elaine's the one who wants to coo at the baby. I want to bait you into a fistfight."

"Jesus Christ." Leo gazes at the ceiling, then laughs. "If you come for dinner, I should ask Daphne and Emerson." He looks at me, considering. "What about you and Finn? Do you have plans?"

"I don't know. I can find out." I'm giddy at the prospect of finding out. It's just a tentative dinner invitation to Leo's, but it feels like a gift. "What about everybody else?"

"Depends on how Haley feels. I can invite Sophia and Tiernan and Lizzy if she's up to a circus."

"It can be a *calm* circus." We reach the big

front doors.

He snorts. "Sure."

"I'm going to text Finn right now." I rest my hand on the push bar and slip my phone out of my purse. Leo puts his hand on the frame above mine, and the door opens. I take a step onto the sidewalk, tapping at the screen. "It would be nice if—"

"Ms. Morelli!" The shout is loud and close. My body jolts from the volume. "Ms. Morelli, do you have anything to say about the Hughes conspiracy?"

Paparazzi crowd in, filling the sidewalk. I can't see my SUV over their heads, or my security.

A hand comes down on my shoulder. Leo's. It holds me in place while both my brothers launch themselves in front of me. I take a step back toward the glassed-in doors.

"Step away," Lucian snaps, voice icy. "She doesn't have a comment."

Leo shoves his open palms in the direction of the photographers, forcing them back. They keep surging forward as he snarls at them, a vicious smile on his face.

"What the fuck do you think you're doing? No, please, take another step. I'll consider you a threat to my sister's life if you move one more inch."

The cameras don't stop flashing. Security has arrived, but they're on the outside of the crush, having to shove their way through. I'm in the only clear pocket of space behind Leo and Lucian.

They keep repeating that we have no comment. The questions don't stop. Some of them are aimed at my brothers.

"Did you know your fiancé was covering up his father's dementia? Eva. Over here. How much did the rest of the family know about this? Is Morelli Holdings involved? Eva. This way. Were you helping him to hide it? Is your engagement a plot to distract the public from the conspiracy?"

My face feels bloodless and numb. Two minutes ago, we were making dinner plans. I was so happy. I was going to find out if Finn was free.

He's not going to be free now that the news is out.

I don't have any idea how it happened. I can hardly breathe.

Our respective security teams converge, finally surrounding us. They make a path through the rowdy clutch of shouting men and women with telephoto lenses. Someone opens the back door of my SUV and I climb in. Leo stands in front of it, blocking me from the photographers. Lucian's right next to him.

One of the agents moves to shut the door behind me.

He's not quite fast enough.

A final shouted question breaks through:

"What about your baby? Does your baby have the disease, too?"

Thank you for reading the emotional story of Finn and Eva. Find out whether the Hughes curse is real in the explosive next book, THREE TO GET READY…

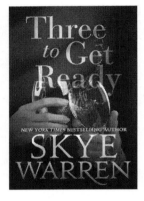

There's a ticking clock over Finn Hughes head.

It's only a matter of time. That means he has to prepare everyone. Eva. The baby. The company, which is in an uproar after the announcement. He needs to get them ready because when the curse hits, it will be too late to say goodbye.

Other books about the Morelli family include:

- Lucian and Elaine in HEARTLESS
- Tiernan and Bianca in DANGEROUS TEMPTATION
- Sophia and Damon in CLAIM

The warring Morelli and Constantine families have enough bad blood to fill an ocean, and their brand new stories will be told by your favorite dangerous romance authors. See what books are available now and sign up to get notified about new releases here…

www.dangerouspress.com

ABOUT MIDNIGHT DYNASTY

The warring Morelli and Constantine families have enough bad blood to fill an ocean, and their brand new stories will be told by your favorite dangerous romance authors.

Meet the oldest Morelli brother in his own star-crossed story...

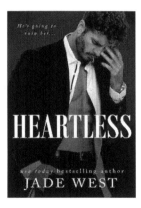

I've known all my life that the Constantines deserved to be wiped from the face of the earth, only a smoking crater left where their mansion once stood. That's my plan until I see her, the woman in gold with the sinful curves and the blonde curls.

In a single moment, she becomes my obsession...

Elaine Constantine will be mine. And her destruction is only my beginning.

My will to dominate her runs as deep as the

hate I have for her last name. No matter how beautifully she bends beneath my hands, I'll leave her shattered, a broken toy for her cruel family.

Winston Constantine is the head of the Constantine family. He's used to people bowing to his will. Money can buy anything. And anyone. Including Ash Elliot, his new maid.

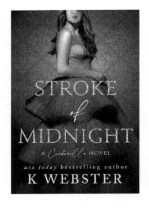

But love can have deadly consequences when it comes from a Constantine. At the stroke of midnight, that choice may be lost for both of them.

"Brilliant storytelling packed with a powerful emotional punch, it's been years since I've been so invested in a book. Erotic romance at its finest!"

— #1 New York Times bestselling author Rachel Van Dyken

"Stroke of Midnight is by far the hottest book I've read in a very long time! Winston Constantine is a dirty talking alpha who makes no apologies for going after what he wants."

Ready for more bad boys, more drama, and more heat? The Constantines have a resident fixer. The man they call when they need someone persuaded in a violent fashion. Ronan was danger and beauty, murder and mercy.

Outside a glittering party, I saw a man in the dark. I didn't know then that he was an assassin. A hit man. A mercenary. Ronan radiated danger and beauty. Mercy and mystery.

I wanted him, but I was already promised to another man. Ronan might be the one who murdered him. But two warring families want my blood. I don't know where to turn.

In a mad world of luxury and secrets, he's the only one I can trust.

"M. O'Keefe brings her A-game in this sexy, complicated romance where you're left questioning if everything you thought was true while dying to get your hands on the next book!"

> – New York Times bestselling author
> K. Bromberg

SIGN UP FOR THE NEWSLETTER
www.dangerouspress.com

JOIN THE FACEBOOK GROUP HERE
www.dangerouspress.com/facebook

FOLLOW US ON INSTAGRAM
www.instagram.com/dangerouspress

About Skye Warren

Skye Warren is the New York Times bestselling author of dangerous romance such as the Endgame trilogy. Her books have been featured in Jezebel, Buzzfeed, USA Today Happily Ever After, Glamour, and Elle Magazine. She makes her home in Texas with her loving family, sweet dogs, and evil cat.

Sign up for Skye's newsletter:
www.skyewarren.com/newsletter

Like Skye Warren on Facebook:
facebook.com/skyewarren

Join Skye Warren's Dark Room reader group:
skyewarren.com/darkroom

Follow Skye Warren on Instagram:
instagram.com/skyewarrenbooks

Visit Skye's website for her current booklist:
www.skyewarren.com

COPYRIGHT

Printed in Great Britain
by Amazon